Jack Bolt and the
HIGHWAYMEN'S
HIDEOUT

Also by Richard Hamilton and Sam Hearn

Cal and the Amazing Anti-Gravity Machine
Violet and the Mean and Rotten Pirates

Jack Bolt and the HIGHWAYMEN'S HIDEOUT

Richard Hamilton

illustrated by Sam Hearn

BLOOMSBURY
CHILDREN'S
BOOKS

First published in Great Britain by Bloomsbury Publishing Plc
Published in the United States by Bloomsbury U.S.A. Children's Books
175 Fifth Avenue, New York, NY 10010
Distributed to the trade by Holtzbrinck Publishers

Library of Congress Cataloging-in-Publication Data
Hamilton, Richard.
Jack Bolt and the highwaymen's hideout / by Richard Hamilton ;
illustrations by Sam Hearn.—1st U.S. ed.
p.   cm.
Summary: While staying at his grandmother's home, Jack finds a hole into the
eighteenth century when a band of highwaymen tumble into his bedroom.
ISBN-13: 978-1-59990-090-2 • ISBN-10: 1-59990-090-4 (hardcover)
ISBN-13: 978-1-59990-091-9 • ISBN-10: 1-59990-091-2 (paperback)
[1. Time travel—Fiction. 2. Robbers and outlaws—Fiction. 3. Grandmothers—Fiction.]
I. Hearn, Sam, ill. II. Title.
PZ7.H182658Jac 2007   [Fic]—dc22   2006027977

First U.S. Edition 2007
Typeset by Dorchester Typesetting Group Ltd
Printed in the U.S.A. by Quebecor World Fairfield
2 4 6 8 10 9 7 5 3 1 (hardcover)
2 4 6 8 10 9 7 5 3 1 (paperback)

All papers used by Bloomsbury U.S.A. are natural, recyclable products
made from wood grown in well-managed forests. The manufacturing processes
conform to the environmental regulations of the country of origin.

For my mother —R. H.

To Richard, Di, Imogen, and Phoebe
and also to the genius of William Hogarth
—S. H.

Contents

Chapter One
Lying in Wait

"**H**ow *dare* they be late?" Lord Henry Vane exclaimed, peering at his watch in the moonlight. "We've been waiting for *ages*! My feet are aching, and my hair has gnats in it!"

He waved his glove at the clouds of tiny flies that were swarming around them. Beneath him, his mare, Red Ruby, sighed, her belly filling with air that she expelled with a satisfying snort.

"Brrrrrhhhhhhhh!"

Beside him, his servant, Tom Drum, was seated on a small pony, scratching himself like a dog with fleas.

"It's bloomin' rude, my lord," he agreed. "Here we

are, about to rob the London coach, and they have the nerve to be late! It is very bad manners."

"Stop scratching yourself, man. It makes me want to scratch myself." Lord Henry stood up in his stirrups and scratched his legs vigorously.

Tom Drum took out a long-barreled pistol and reached behind his head to scratch his back with it. "I can't help it, sir. It's the thicket. It's alive."

Lord Henry lit a clay pipe and blew clouds of smoke around them. "That's fixed 'em!" he said, his eyes watering from the smoke. He continued sucking and puffing as together the two highwaymen

watched the lonely moonlit road in front of them. Lord Henry's face was periodically lit up by the red glow of the pipe. He had a large nose and chin, a mole on one cheek, a huge wig of brown curls topped with a three-cornered hat—and on his face, a mask. In the corner of the mask, a red ruby glimmered.

"*Because* they are so late," he told Tom Drum, "we shall rob them of everything tonight. Trinkets, jewelry, hats, furs, lace, and every piece of money. It is our reward for waiting for so long in this wretched swamp. The only things we shall leave the passengers are their watches!"

"But watches is valuable, my lord." Tom Drum was mystified.

"It's a joke, Tom. So they will not be late again, they must have their watches!"

"Oh—ha, ha! Wittily done, my lord. Ha, ha!"

"Thank you, Tom."

"May I request a nice pair of new boots? My current ones has holes in the soles."

"By all means."

"And a new undershirt. I need a new undershirt." Tom Drum scratched himself under his arm.

"Do you?"

"Yes, my lord. And pants. I need new pants. In

fact—I require a whole new set of silken under-clothes!"

"Really? But, Tom—this would mean they had no clothes on. It is not gentlemanly to steal a man's undergarments. We cannot leave them naked on the highway in the moonlight!"

"No? I thought you said we would rob them of everything?"

"It was a joke, remember? No, no, it is quite wrong to steal their underwear." Lord Henry was troubled.

"They could have *my* undergarments," Tom suggested. "We could swap. Mine are basic but quite serviceable."

"No, Tom. It is *unthinkable*." Lord Henry waved his pipe at the tiny flies. "When people sing ballads about us a hundred years from now, I don't want to be known as the highwayman who stole underclothes. A man's reputation is of paramount importance."

Tom Drum frowned. "What's that mean? Paramount?"

"It means 'the very highest.' My reputation is of the very highest importance. Remember: we always treat our victims with courtesy; we are always polite and well mannered. We show them tenderness,

12

concern, *love*. We charm them until they are . . . until they are *grateful* to be robbed! And if possible, we make sure they have a fine story to recount to their friends in society. We want people to *want* to be robbed!"

Lord Henry chuckled. What a marvelously mad idea: to *want* to be robbed! He sucked on his pipe and, finding it was empty, dropped it into his saddle-bag. Underneath him, Red Ruby shifted gently.

"Look!" Tom Drum suddenly grabbed Lord Henry's arm and pointed. "There they are!"

In the distance was a speck, like a black beetle, moving through the moonlit countryside. It disappeared behind trees, and the highwaymen waited and watched.

"That's them," said Lord Henry as the coach appeared again. "At last!" Pleasure and excitement rang in his voice. He took out a little pocket mirror and checked his mask and his white teeth. Satisfied, he put the mirror away and brought out his pistol. He kissed it. "I see a fine supper ahead! Wine and stew at the old Cap and Stockings. And then a game of cards. Hmm?"

"Aye," agreed Tom Drum, grinning lopsidedly. "So—just the coat and boots, then?"

"And the money!" Lord Henry reminded him.

"And the money," repeated Tom Drum. They took their positions by the road.

"And the necklaces."

"Oh, yes: necklaces, money, coats, and boots . . ."

The coach lurched toward them—two lanterns like yellow eyes, blinking in the silvery night. With a clatter of hooves the highwaymen rode up onto the road and stopped the coach.

Lord Henry waved his pistol in the air. He shouted out in a fine, full voice:

> *"Stand and deliver!*
> *Lord Henry Vane is my name,*
> *And highway robbery is my game!"*

Chapter Two
Mysterious Voices

Far away across the heath, Jack couldn't sleep. He always found it difficult to sleep in Granny's house. Maybe it was the light: moonlight streaming through the thin white curtains, giving the room a wash of cold silver. Or maybe it was the musty smell. Granny never used the guest room, so the air was stale, with a hint of mothballs and furniture polish.

He turned over and looked at the clock. The red lights glowed: 10:30. Half past ten. At home Mom and Dad would be watching TV. Just like Granny downstairs. *That's what grown-ups do after they put you to bed*, he thought. *They go downstairs and watch TV.*

Sometimes they act like they're doing something else—something important—which is why they say things like "Go on! Get to bed, we've got things to do." And then they flop down in front of the flickering screen. He turned over again. Boing! A spring twanged in the mattress.

That was the other reason Jack couldn't sleep: the bed. This was the noisiest bed in the world! Every time he moved, the springs sprang. Twang! Boing! Pingggggg! It was like lying on a harp. Or on the strings of a grand piano. And the head-board creaked like a door in a horror movie. Errrrreeeeeeerrrrrrrrrrr!

He decided he would lie as still as possible so that the bed made no noise at all. Not a creak. Not a ping or a twang *at all*. He would count to see how long he could go without moving . . .

He looked at the dark shapes of the furniture looming around him: the chest of drawers, the tall-backed armchair, the old seaman's chest. They all looked sinister—he tried not to let himself become frightened by them. It was as if he was sharing his room with black lumps from which monsters might erupt.

This was the first time Jack had stayed at his

granny's house on his own, without his parents. They had had to stay in London to work. He wondered what he would do. It was only three days and nights, but he had no friends here, no computer, no games, nothing. It was going to be really boring. And Granny was permanently busy.

Then again, that might be a good thing. He liked the freedom Granny gave him. She had a straightforward policy when it came to ten-year-old visitors: she believed that they were quite capable of looking after themselves. She was there only for emergencies. "Food and first aid," she'd said to him. "Your room is for you. It's your private place. Do what you like. I will not come in unless specially invited!"

And she didn't, either. She insisted on talking to him from outside the room, in the hall. As she was a little deaf, this wasn't always easy. "Grown-ups have privacy—why shouldn't children?" she had said. "Now, good-bye—I've got things to do." She always had things to do: the parish council, the village museum, visiting the sick. She spent a lot of time in the kitchen writing letters or cursing her typewriter, always, of course, keeping a sharp eye out for the neighbors. Her little cottage was in the middle of the pretty village, looking out over a square with benches and trees and other little old houses, and she knew everyone.

Jack might have drifted off to sleep then, listening gently to nothing in particular—the occasional car passing, voices in the square below—and lying so still that the creaky bed was silent. But suddenly he heard a shout, and his eyes sprang open.

"Soldiers?" cried a woman's voice. "Hey! Where do you think you're going?"

Jack sat up in bed and looked out of the window. Doinggg! The bedsprings sprang. The little square was quiet. Some of the old houses had lights on blinking through the leaves on the trees. The cars were parked. The bench in the middle of the square was empty. The Cap and Stockings pub across the street had a light on.

"We have orders to check every room!" Jack heard a man say gruffly.

He thought there must be someone in the hall.

There was a stamping of feet on the stairs and a sudden kick and a crash. Jack stared at his bedroom door. But no one came in. Still he tried to work out where the voices were coming from. Somewhere in the house—maybe in the kitchen beneath his

room? He looked nervously at the black shapes of
the furniture.

"We're looking for the Vane Gang," the man said
loudly. "They're robbing every traveler on the road,
and Parliament has had enough."

"But he's the posh Toby," objected the woman.
She seemed to be on the other side of the wall.
"He's never hurt anyone. And they say he is terribly
handsome!"

"Ha!" The man laughed hollowly.

"I wouldn't mind getting robbed by him meself!"
the woman joked.

"Oh, yeah?" The man's voice had a threatening edge to it. "You like him, do you? You think it is all right to steal, do you?"

"Oh, no!" replied the woman quickly. "He should be hanged. They all should be hanged."

"Yeah," the man said cruelly. "He'll dance upon nothing soon enough."

Jack heard a door slam, then footsteps and silence. It was suddenly so quiet that he could hear his heart beating. He swallowed. Was Granny all right? When he thought the coast was clear, he slipped out of bed and went to investigate. He tiptoed through the dark house—but he found everything as it should be. Granny was watching TV. The landing and hall were empty. The doors and windows were shut. Looking down the street one way and into the village square the other way, there was nothing suspicious, nothing unusual.

He tiptoed back to bed. Had he imagined it? Could it be a ghost—a spirit in the room? The last words rang in Jack's head: "He'll dance upon nothing soon enough."

What did it mean?

Chapter Three
A Great Honor

"Ladies and gentlemen! You have the great honor to be robbed by the one and only Lord Henry Vane!" The highwayman twirled his pistol in the air and made Red Ruby rear up on her hind legs. She did it very elegantly, as if it were a little exclamation mark at the end of the highwayman's speech.

"As you are late tonight—and have much inconvenienced me—I will be removing one item of clothing from each of you and distributing it to the poor of the parish!" Henry Vane announced. "Pray come out."

The coach driver opened the carriage door and

the first passenger stepped out. Henry Vane held up a lantern. It was a stout woman with a wide bonnet and a silvery shawl wrapped around her.

"Are you suggesting I take off my dress?" she asked coldly.

"Certainly not, madam!" Lord Henry had standards. "Your rings, madam. Your necklace—what a pretty one it is—your shawl, and the silver buckles on your delightful shoes. Collect them, Tom."

Tom Drum slid off his horse and approached the woman. He bent a little, like a fawning butler, as she reluctantly gave him the jewelry and stood aside.

Next came a scowling young man with a black traveling cloak, boots, and a hat pulled low over his face. He held out a small bag.

"It's all I have," he said, trembling. He blinked behind his gold-rimmed glasses.

"Thank you," said Lord Henry. "How awfully kind. And I would have your cloak for the poor."

"And the boots, my lord," said Tom Drum, looking up eagerly to Henry Vane. "Them's a nice pair."

"Yes, yes, the boots too. Take them off."

"My boots?" asked the young man. "But what will I wear?"

"We'll swap!" Tom Drum told him. Hopping around the coach, Tom Drum pulled off his own boots. They had holes in them and one sole flapped. He thrust them in the young man's arms and snatched the man's boots off him. "Much obliged. I reckon they is a perfect fit!"

The two highwaymen laughed. Lord Henry proceeded with the robbery.

"Come on—don't be shy. Would the next passenger step forward, please. Now, listen up: I am praying for some lovely, plump money bags . . ."

"Ooooo, yes." Tom Drum did a little dance in his new boots.

Chapter Four
The Knife in the Wall

In the middle of the night, Jack woke up. The clock showed 3:33. For a moment he wondered where he was. Then he realized: in Granny's guest room, surrounded by the dark furniture. Something had woken him up, startled him out of his sleep. What could it be? He remembered the voices of the woman and the soldier.

He didn't want to, but he forced himself to look around the room. He told himself that if he looked carefully, he was bound to see nothing—nothing bad, nothing unusual—and that would mean everything was all right.

But as he peered into the darkness, he heard a

scratching noise coming from the wall. It startled him and sent a tingle up his spine. Was it an animal—a rat maybe, or a mouse, in the wall? He stared in the direction of the noise, squinting his eyes into the darkness. And suddenly he saw something that made his blood run cold.

A knife. Sliding through the wall. He saw its silver blade sawing through the wallpaper. Noisier now, scratching and tearing. In and out. Glinting for a moment, and then dull gray. It seemed to be making an opening.

Jack's mouth was open; he wanted to call out, but he couldn't.

He watched as the knife cut three sides of a square—an "n" shape. The bottom of the "n" was the floor. It was about two feet square, big enough to crawl through.

And then to Jack's horror, the wallpaper fell away, leaving a dark, square, empty hole.

Jack saw something come through the hole, something the size of a small animal, and he let out a tiny cry.

"What's that?" whispered someone. A man's voice.

It was quickly answered.

"The pigs. The pigs is down below."

Now Jack saw a hand coming through into his room. It had a loose white cuff and was holding a canvas bag. The hand put the bag down in the room. There was a muffled clang of metal objects banging together, and then the hand withdrew and the wallpaper was put back in place. It was like a little door opening out of his room, with hinges at the bottom on the floor.

Who would put a bag in his room?

He was just about to force himself to get out of bed and tiptoe over to see what had been left, when he heard more whispering on the other side of the wall.

"Strike a light, Tom, for my eyes do play tricks on me!"

Slowly, inch by inch, the hole opened again. There was a flickering light and Jack saw two eyes appear. They were eerie, lit from below by candle-light. Thick, dark eyebrows twitched together.

The eyes swiveled around Jack's room, staring in disbelief.

"Well, blimey!" the man whispered. "Knock me right off my horse and into the ditch!"

The gap widened and the rest of the man's face appeared.

"Knock me backward from Barnstaple and up Frampton Lane! That's a big cupboard! I say, Tom. Look."

A second face appeared. It was round and quizzical with a strange curtain of dark hair hanging over its

forehead. Both men wore old-fashioned triangular hats.

"You see—it is not just a cupboard: it is an entire room!"

"Cockles and codfish! It's huge!" exclaimed the second man, and they both tried to squeeze through at the same time. Jack didn't move.

"Me first," said the man with the long curly hair. "Hog's breath, I just burned my wig!"

"Sorry, sir."

Jack couldn't move. Caught between astonishment and fear, he watched as the man with the wig crawled through the hole in the wall into his bedroom. He held a candle and was dressed in a long waistcoat with an extravagant lace cravat, white riding breeches, and black leather boots. Incredibly, his eyes passed right over Jack, sitting in his bed in the shadows.

"This hidden cupboard is large enough for ten men to hide in. The soldiers would never find us. Not in a month of Sundays." The tall man spoke with pleasure.

"The soldiers could be having a cup of tea downstairs and not know we was here!" laughed the second man. "This room is above the pigs!"

"Impossible!"

"Oh, my lord! This is witchcraft!" The short man shuddered.

"Rubbish—"

"It is a terrible magic," he whimpered.

The tall man now held up the candle. He looked from the curtains to the closet to the bed—and suddenly he locked eyes with Jack.

"BAH! Dash it—a BOY! Whaaaaa!"

He dropped the candle, which hit the floor and went out, plunging them into darkness.

"Get off! My lord! Whaaaaa!"

There was a snap, a thud, and a splintering of wood as the two men fell over and smashed the chair. Panic seized them and there was another bump as one of them blundered into the closet.

Jack leaned out of bed. There was no time to think. He turned on the bedside light.

Click.

Light burst on to the scene, as shocking as an explosion.

The men froze. The tall one with the curly hair and the fine cravat was sprawled on the broken chair, his eyes popping with surprise; the short scruffy man was caught up in the curtain, holding it so hard that there was a slow plinking noise as he pulled it from the hooks. Plink, plink, plink.

In the bright light, they were both thoroughly exposed.

"Who are you?" stammered the tall man.

"I'm Jack Bolt," said Jack, with a steely control. He breathed deeply, evenly. He was worried his voice might falter. "Who are you?"

The tall man lay blinking in the light—he gazed at it with deep suspicion as he struggled noisily to his feet. He brushed himself off and adjusted his wig. At last he announced in a hushed, self-important tone: "I am Lord Henry Vane. Highwayman of glorious fame. Your servant," he said with a bow.

"And I," said the man still gripping the curtain, "I am Tom Drum. *His* servant."

Chapter Five
A Loop in the Ribbon of Time

"Jack! Are you all right in there?" It was Granny, calling from the landing.

"Yes."

"What did you say?"

"YES, Granny!"

"I heard a bump—"

"I'm okay! I fell out of bed."

"You fell on your head?"

"BED! I fell out of BED."

"Oh, good. I'm going to bed, too."

Jack didn't tell his granny about the visitors. His first thought was to call out, to get her to come in and rescue him, but then the tall man—Henry Vane—glared at him and put his finger to his lips. Jack understood: this was a threat. Then the man took out an antique pistol. This was a serious threat.

"Good night, Granny!" Jack called.

"Good night."

Henry Vane smiled. It was quite a friendly smile, for someone holding a pistol. "Good boy, Jack Bolt," he said in a low voice. His eyes were drawn to the light by Jack's bed. He gazed at it as if it were some dangerous magic.

"What are you doing in my bedroom?" Jack asked.

"No, Jack Bolt," retorted Henry Vane, adjusting his hair, "what are *you* doing in *my* . . . cupboard?" He stroked his cheek with the antique pistol in a thoughtful way.

"Looks like a bedroom to me," Jack replied. *These men are weird*, Jack thought. *All dressed up as if from another century*. Despite the threatening pistol, there was something almost funny about them. It was as if they had stepped off a stage or out of a movie screen. It was strange: for some reason they appeared confused and frightened by Jack. That was good, he thought; it gave him courage.

Lord Henry Vane's nostrils quivered. He kept looking around the room as if he couldn't believe his eyes. He obviously didn't like being contradicted. "It's a cupboard," he insisted, stubborn in the face of the evidence. "A large cupboard, almost like a room. Beside the fireplace in Nanny Manners's house."

"With a bed," Jack pointed out, "and a closet and a chest." He didn't have a clue who this Nanny Manners might be. "I'm telling you: you are in *my* granny's house, where I am staying."

". . . In the cupboard above . . . the . . . pigs . . ." The man by the window, Tom Drum, seemed panicky. His hands were trembling.

For a moment Jack wondered if they were a crazy historical reenactment group, like the ones he'd seen at a castle once. Enthusiasts who liked to dress up in clothes from the past and do spear-fighting demonstrations . . . or maybe this was some awful TV hoax?

Tom Drum took Lord Henry's arm. "Consider, my lord," he whispered, "that this is not a boy? Eh? This is an *angel*?" He pointed a dirty finger at Jack. "Look at his pearly skin and strange yellow hair. And his garments . . . *what* are they?"

Jack glanced down at his pajamas. They had a

winged motif on the front and the words "Motor-cycle Heaven" printed in a gothic script. His pajama bottoms were plain red cotton. What was wrong with his skin? At least it was clean—these guys looked like they needed a shave and a serious wash.

"No. He's got no wings," said Lord Henry, peering at Jack as if he were a freak.

Jack didn't like being a curiosity. Especially when *they* were the strange ones.

"When you say that you're a highwayman," he asked as casually as he could, "do you mean that you are robbers?"

Both men smiled, which unnerved Jack. Tom Drum had a gap-toothed grin; Lord Henry had a wide, white, winning smile—the too-good-to-be-true, heart-melting smile of a charmer.

"We are robbers," Henry Vane told him grandly, puffing himself up like a peacock. "But no ordinary foot padders: we are gentlemen robbers, on horse-back. There's a world of difference." He picked up Jack's toothbrush and idly studied it. He'd never seen one before. What was its use, he wondered.

"Well, you're housebreakers now," Jack pointed out.

"Watch it, boy!" Lord Henry's smile vanished. He stabbed the air with the toothbrush, pointing it at

Jack. "Housebreakers are very low. Highwaymen have considerably more standing! *They* are sneaky; *we* are daring!" He tossed the threatening toothbrush aside; it landed silently on the bed.

"Sorrrreee," said Jack. *They're quick to take offense*, he thought. "Where are you from?" he asked.

"Here and there," replied Henry Vane, running his fingers through the frill on the edge of the lampshade. "We appear out of the darkness when we are least expected. And where are *you* from, Jack Bolt?"

"London," Jack replied straightforwardly.

"But that's not London speech." Henry Vane raised an eyebrow.

"Well, I live there."

"Where, exactly?" The highwayman challenged him.

"Holloway. Near the subway station."

"Holloway-near-the-subway-station? I know London—and I know it well—and there is no such place," he asserted, his eyes narrowing. Before Jack could reply, there was an outburst from Tom Drum at the window.

"Lord a' mercy! Look, my lord! The houses—they have multiplied. The pigs . . . gone! The cooper's house and Old Ma Cracklepot's—gone!

Oh, my lord—we have been bad and now some wicked spell is on us."

"What are you squawking about, Tom?" In a stride Lord Henry joined Tom at the window and looked out. He clasped his hand to his heart.

"Blood and thunder!" he swore. "'Tis London! No—look: there is the Cap and Stockings. But—all else is changed! So many houses. And lights. Maybe you are right, Tom—the devil is abroad! Where can this be—Jack, tell me!" he demanded.

"The village? It is called Wittlesham." Their tone made Jack uneasy. He began to feel dizzy, as if a great space had opened in his head.

Lord Henry nodded. He breathed deeply, in and out. He seemed to struggle with an idea and for the words to express it. "It is Wittlesham—but—the farms are gone, the houses altered . . ."

Through the dizziness, a thought came to Jack—and the world seemed to somersault: these men were not pretending to be from the past. They *were* from the past—he knew it.

"What date is it—where you are from?" His voice shook.

"The thirtieth of October."

"No—the year. What year is it?"

The men looked at each other and at Jack. "Year of our Lord: 1752."

"Really?" Jack asked, his eyes wide. "I mean *really REALLY*?"

"Indeed. Really, REALLY," replied Henry Vane, bristling. His hand slowly rose to his brow.

"You are now at the beginning of the twenty-first century!" Jack exclaimed. "You have traveled forward in time over *two hundred and fifty years!*"

The men did not understand. Jack watched their faces struggle with the idea.

"Piffle!" said Lord Henry at last.

"What does that mean—'traveled forward in time'?" Tom Drum was bewildered. His mouth

opened in a big O. "On what?"

"It is a monstrous idea," said Lord Henry. "An abomination!"

But Jack was now convinced. "It happens all the time in the movies," he told them excitedly.

"The whats?" Tom Drum was mystified.

"And on TV."

"On what?"

"It could never happen." Lord Henry looked desperately around the room. "Impossible."

"Did you have electric lights like this—or toothbrushes—or plastic bags or footballs—or ballpoint pens—did you have them in 1752?"

The men were silent. Henry Vane's eyes darted around the room. He stared at the things Jack pointed to.

"Did you have cars and trains and planes?"

The men frowned. They did not understand such things.

"Did you have—"

Lord Henry held up his hand, looking back at the hole in the wall through which they had appeared and then to the room where they were standing. His voice shook. "It may be that some strange thing has happened—that time is out of joint and all awry—I know not. Nor does it matter. But, but this I do know . . ."

"*How* is it, my lord?" interrupted Tom Drum, holding his head as if the thought hurt. "I don't understand!"

"Imagine, Tom, a ribbon." Henry dug around in his pockets and pulled out a black ribbon, which he held up like a magician. "A long ribbon of time. Think of the years stretching out across its length. And then suddenly the ribbon doubles back on itself and two parts—two different times—touch." A confidence lit up Lord Henry's eyes as he made a loop in the ribbon. "Our time and Jack's time have touched. Now—we are in that loop and somehow, *somehow*, we have passed through from one time to the other. Is it so?" he asked Jack.

"In a nutshell." Jack grinned at the elegance of the explanation as his mind reeled with the possibilities.

"Yet it matters not one bit . . . for this," continued Henry Vane, delighting in a brilliant idea that was just dawning on him, "this is *the very best hide-out in the land*. Why, Ali Baba couldn't have wished for a better cave to hide his loot in! And Jack, Jack Bolt . . . the Keeper of the Hideout—you will keep our secret, eh? You will look after our loot? For we shall pay you *handsomely* for the use of your bed-room! In golden guineas and so forth. Only you must tell no one. Eh? Not even the granny—what do you say?"

"Okay," Jack said guardedly. He wasn't sure if this was the right thing to do, but he had no choice.

"O. K." Henry Vane frowned. "O. K.? Is that yes or no? I have no 'O. K.'"

"It's 'yes,'" said Jack.

"Then we bid you a good night, Jack Bolt," said Lord Henry abruptly. He bowed elaborately, then backed out through the hole, pushing Tom Drum through first. "We have work to do, Jack—important work. But we shall be back. We shall be back," he said and winked as he closed the hole in the wall.

Jack lay still in his bed. He waited until there was silence, then stepped over to where the strange men had disappeared. The wallpaper was torn and messy, as they had crawled over it from the other side. *It must be some sort of door*, he thought and gave it a push.

It wouldn't budge.

Chapter Six
The Other Time

"I've got a very busy day, I'm afraid," said Jack's granny at breakfast the following morning. "And I expect you do too?"

She looked at Jack with beady eyes. She always made him feel that she could see right through him. Her gray hair was cut short and her beaky nose and blinking eyes made Jack think of a smart bird. She had provided a hearty breakfast of oatmeal and a boiled egg and toast. Now she was expecting an answer.

"I've got a lot to do," Jack told her loudly.

"Good," boomed Granny.

Jack chewed his toast. *I had a couple of highwaymen*

in my bedroom last night. They popped through from the eighteenth century. He practiced saying it in his head. He could say it now. Obviously Granny wouldn't believe him. And then he could take her up and show her . . . what? The mess?

"You know how to reach me," said Granny. My cell phone number is by the phone. I'll be back for lunch. If you get hungry—help yourself. There's ham and quiche in the fridge."

Jack opened his mouth as if to say something, then closed it. Sometimes busy grown-ups miss the most exciting things.

Back in his room, Jack looked at the mess. There were black footprints on the wallpaper, and the candle had made a waxy splotch on the bed. The chair was broken and the curtains were ripped off their hooks. Oh, dear. What would Granny say?

Then he saw the bag that the highwaymen had left, lying by the old chest. In all the excitement, he had missed it. He opened the drawstring and looked inside. There were silver knives and a silver jug, a bag of coins, and some rings and a necklace. Wow! Treasure! Real treasure.

He reexamined the wall. First thing in the

morning he had tried again to open it. He had picked at the wallpaper and found a sheet of rusty metal with hinges at the bottom. He had pushed it, but it wouldn't move. He wondered—had it always been here—only just now discovered?

Looking again, he thought he could see a sliver of light at the side. He found a metal coat hanger and began working the hook along the top edge, sawing in and out as the knife had done the previous night. Suddenly the door fell open. "Yes!" Jack clenched his fist in triumph. Then, blinking through a small cloud of dust and plaster, he peered through.

The metal door had fallen to the side of a fireplace on the other side of the wall. As the dust settled, he could see into the room beyond. It was a room he had never seen before.

Smaller than the room in Granny's house, it was darker and dirtier. Jack could see a rough, unmade bed and a wooden chair with clothes on it. He felt fluttering butterflies in his stomach. Could he really be on the brink of the eighteenth century?

Then the smell hit him. Wood smoke and pigs! It stuck in his throat and made his eyes water. Still, he took a deep breath and crawled through. The whole world changed. The house was suddenly utterly

silent, as if the low buzzing of modern life had been wiped clean away. Here was a deep country silence, without electronics or machines or passing aircraft.

He found the room basic and bare. There was a small window low down on his left. On his right, there was a candle on the floor with a cascade of drips around it. A black coat hung on a hook by the narrow door. It felt like a different house.

Gradually he became aware of sounds. He heard a crowing far off, a squawking of birds, a grunting and snuffling of pigs. It was as if he was in a farm-yard. A voice outside startled him. The accent was so broad and unfamiliar that he couldn't make out what was being said. It sounded like: "Saaaf. In the faaarrrmy."

He peeped out of the dirty little window.

"Oh, wicked!" he breathed. The view from his bedroom window, of the little market square with trees and benches and a clean black road running around neat little houses and shops, was completely transformed. There was mud everywhere. The houses were small and dirty. Ducks and hens roamed freely; a horse and cart stood waiting.

But there was the pub! The Cap and Stockings! It was immediately recognizable with its row of three dormer windows and the jutting-out window by the door. It was dirtier and poorer and had ivy growing up one side, but it was unmistakably the same building.

A man appeared at the far end of the square. He was wearing a smock and rough peasant clothes. Jack watched him put a wooden box on the cart, then he disappeared around the corner of a building. An everyday scene of the eighteenth century—just a man loading a cart.

Jack crept to the door of the room, past the unmade bed and a leather bag stuffed with clothes that spilled out onto the floor. He saw the arm of a man's shirt trailing across the floorboards, and he caught a glimpse of a gold button nestled in dark folds of velvet. He couldn't help feeling he was in an entirely different house but had to remind himself that he wasn't. This was still Granny's house! So he wasn't doing anything wrong, was he?

He opened the small door and found a narrow staircase. There was no staircase here in Granny's house. But it must lead down to the kitchen. Jack listened. Nothing. The first steps creaked dreadfully. As he expected, there was the kitchen, smaller and darker than Granny's. Looking through the simple oak banister, he could see a table and two chairs and the big fireplace with a fire slumbering and pots and pans stacked nearby.

Jack stepped off the last stair. And something hit him.

Chapter Seven
A Knotty Problem

Thrown to the floor, Jack was plunged into darkness, clutching the side of his head. Someone pulled a hood over his face. He tried to cry out but he couldn't, as the cloth was jammed in his mouth and someone was on top of him, grappling with his arms.

"Shut up, thief, or I'll slit yer throat like a pig!" a high voice hissed into his ear.

Jack struggled but he wasn't used to fighting and found himself quickly overpowered. Before he knew what had happened, he was tied up and forced into a chair. His arms wouldn't budge. Whoever it was didn't want him to escape. A rope was wound round and round and round the chair until Jack was covered from his neck to his ankles. He felt angry and hot. Moving his head around, he managed to spit out the cloth in his mouth.

"You don't need to tie me up anymore," he pleaded, coughing.

"Shut up," hissed his attacker. "An' no running off." Jack heard a high laugh, almost a giggle.

"Don't worry—I'm hardly going anywhere," he muttered, blinking in the darkness. He could just make out slivers of light here and there.

She laughed again. It was the high-pitched laugh of a girl! Worse—she was smaller than he was!

"Please—take the bag off—I . . . I can't . . . breathe . . . ," he complained.

"All right—I'll take off the sack, but ye must not say a word—y'hear?"

Jack grunted. "Okay. I'll be quiet." (*I'll shout the house down if it helps*, he thought.)

The girl took off the bag and Jack saw a fierce little face staring at him with a triumphant glint in her eye. Jack felt anger and humiliation. Whatever had been in the bag had been covered in dirt. He could taste it. The girl must be about his age, he thought. Her face was smudged with dirt, and wisps of hair hung down from a scarf tied behind her ears. She had narrow little eyes and a small nose. She held a poker in her hand.

She grinned. "Got y'all ready for market, eh?" She glanced down at the ropes with satisfaction. "'Though you was a bit more trouble than a turkey!"

She stood back and suddenly kicked him in the shin. Not too hard (and, anyway, he was protected by the thick rope binding), but not playfully either.

"OW."

"Shut up," she growled. "Thief."

"I'm not a thief," Jack said.

"Yes, you are." She glared at him. She seemed about to spit in his face, then thought better of it.

The girl stared at Jack's sneakers. They were new and white. His jeans were a beautiful blue too.

"What were you doing up there, thief?" she asked, jutting out her chin.

"I'm not a thief," he told her again.

She held out the poker and pointed it at him. "Yes, you are. Thief. Or spy?" she added venomously.

"Neither," Jack said. He wanted to say "*I'm a time traveler!*" But he didn't. It was too ridiculous. "I know Lord Henry Vane."

That brought her up short. She frowned and

tilted her head to the side. "Do you, now?" She smiled slyly. "I don't know him meself. Maybe you should be telling the soldiers? For you may see the soldiers shortly, I can tell you."

"Why would I tell the soldiers?" he said. "I'm Lord Henry's friend."

"He's a Toby," she told him.

"A what?"

"A highwayman. You should be careful of the company you keeps. Or you'll be dancing on nothing." She mimed a rope pulling at her neck, kicked her legs, and grinned wickedly at him. Now Jack understood the phrase. "'Oo made your shoes?" she asked, still intrigued by his sneakers.

Before he had time to answer, someone called from outside: "Polly!" It was a woman's voice. The woman he had heard last night with the soldier.

The girl, Polly, left him, hurrying past—her face suddenly hard.

Jack could hear them talking outside in low voices. With a sick feeling he realized that in the eighteenth century they hanged thieves.

A moment later there was a shout from outside, and a short round woman bustled into the kitchen. She had a ruddy face, warts on her chin, and unruly gray hair. She placed her hands on her hips and stared at Jack, all tied up as if he were about to perform an escapology trick.

"Oh, the devil! Look at the knots—you wild child!" It wasn't clear whether she was referring to Jack or to the girl named Polly. "There's no end of trouble here. Who are you?" she demanded, speaking softly to Jack.

Polly hadn't asked him who he was. "I'm Jack Bolt," he said. "And I'm sorry, I didn't know it was your house . . ."

She studied him thoughtfully and spoke quietly again. "So where did you pop up from, Jack Bolt?"

"Next door," he said truthfully.

She squinted at him. Jack felt pinned down by her piercing blue eyes. "Did you, now? She says you know Henry. Is it so?"

Jack nodded—here was an opening. "Sure," he said. "We're old friends."

"Fetch Henry!" the woman told Polly.

"Where—," began Polly.

"Where d'ya think? In the back room at the Cap and Stockings. They been there all night, they have, wasting their money. Tell him young Jack Bolt is here to see him—if he's a mind to come."

51

Polly disappeared and the ruddy-faced woman looked over at Jack and chuckled. "She can tie a knot, that one. She can't cook a sausage, but she can tie a knot like a bargeman."

Lord Henry Vane came with Tom Drum in tow. Polly showed them in and proudly presented Jack. "You see—I'm as good as any man!" she said. To Jack's annoyance, they both burst out laughing.

"Why—if you had caught the world's strongest man, Polly, you could not have tied him up more thoroughly!"

"You know this lad, Henry?" the ruddy-faced woman asked.

"I do indeed, Mistress Manners. He is a valued member of the gang." Henry looked at Jack, but his eyes were cold. "More than that, he is our lucky charm."

"What?" cried Polly indignantly. "Since when is *he* a member of the gang?"

"Since quite recent," Tom Drum told her.

"But you promised me," Polly said to Lord Henry.

"Later, Polly—untie this lad now, please."

As Polly walked around and around Jack, undoing the coils of rope, Jack's feeling of relief drained away. The chiseled features of Lord Henry were sunk deep in thought. Behind his eyes lurked a darkness. He pulled Jack up the stairs and turned on him.

"What do you think you're doing, you turkey?"

"I just wanted to see if it was true—that you came from the eighteenth century. I wanted to see what life was like here," said Jack.

"Life? It's one short cackle of laughter," Lord Henry said with sudden venom. "And then we're off to the other world. Did you tell them about the hideout?"

"No."

"Good lad. We're relying on you." He let go of Jack's arm and grew friendlier. "Let us make a deal, Jack Bolt: you want to see life, then I'll show you life, here in the glorious eighteenth century, but you must help us tonight. I am a suspicious man, Jack—it is my nature—and now that you are here I shall have to keep you nearby, for I can't run the risk of having the hideout discovered. It is a most precious place. Tonight there is a job to be done, if you get my meaning, and afterward we will need a place to rest up. I think it'd be best if you come with us. Don't you?"

Lord Henry smiled. It felt like the sun breaking through the clouds. Jack realized that he had no choice.

Chapter Eight
Taking from the Rich

Clinging to the highwayman's coat, Jack galloped across the countryside. A vast cloud of starlings—more birds than he had ever seen— wheeled in the overcast sky above them. Lord Henry's curly wig was pushed into Jack's face and was maddeningly itchy. He had been given some rough clothes that not only smelled like old cheese but also scratched him raw. It was like wearing an old doormat. His bottom banged on the saddle until it was bruised and sore.

Despite this, Jack felt a fantastic freedom as the air whistled past his ears and the thud of the horses' hooves shuddered through his body. As the countryside sped past he felt like whooping for joy. When Red Ruby leaped over a hedge, Jack's stomach lurched and he clung on for dear, glorious life.

Around him, the countryside wasn't that different from his own time. Of course there were no cars or paved roads, and there were many more trees—but otherwise, it was the same. Sky and fields and woods and lanes and houses. The houses were smaller, and there were hardly any of them. And the roads were only dirt trails. Jack had seen paintings of this old countryside, full of people in the fields and warm colors and horses and distant houses, and it really was like that. He felt freer without the roads and the signs and the fences everywhere. This world felt more open and empty—and more dangerous too.

They came to a halt under an old oak tree on the roadside. Tom Drum trotted up behind them with Polly. She had insisted on coming, and Lord Henry seemed unwilling to stop her. Jack wished she wasn't with them—she either ignored him or shot him glances of hate. He did the same back.

They had waited only a short while when three horsemen came cantering up to them. They wore hats and black cloaks.

"Lord Henry Vane!" called one as he galloped up.

"The very same!" called Lord Henry back. "Well met, lads! Your timing is perfect—we have just arrived."

From behind Lord Henry, Jack looked at the men. They were a fine sight from afar—black figures galloping with their cloaks flying in the wind—but close up, he saw they were rough and shady characters, with bad teeth and tattered clothes.

"This is Dirty Dick," said Lord Henry, gesturing to a bearded man with a hungry look.

Dirty Dick peered at Jack. He said nothing but looked mystified.

"And this is Pete the Pudding."

A stout man nudged his horse forward and also peered at Jack then Polly. "'Ello, young un," he said to Jack.

"Hello," said Polly brightly, before Jack could speak.

"And this is Bernard." Lord Henry gestured to a big man with a thick jaw and a long red scar down his cheek.

"Bad-Breath Bernard," said Dirty Dick.

"Haaaaaaaaaa!" went Bernard in Dirty Dick's direction.

"Woooooooooorrrr! You could wilt a flower in Wessex with your breath!" groaned Dirty Dick, holding his nose.

"An' your fizzle ain't so fragrant neither, Dick," growled Bernard, standing in his stirrups and leaning over.

"And behind me—is Jack Bolt," said Henry swiftly. "Welcome to the Vane Gang!"

"'E's just a boy," observed Dirty Dick.

"So what?" said Polly to Jack's surprise.

"And that's just a girl!" exclaimed Bernard.

Jack noticed two guns sticking out of a belt that Bernard wore across his chest.

"I'm as good as any of you," began Polly, glaring at them. "I can load and shoot a pistol. I've done it lots."

"What you shot, then?" asked Dirty Dick. "A couple of gnats?"

"I shot a duck," said Polly.

"Sittin' on a pond!" laughed Pete the Pudding. His laugh was unfortunate, a stupid-sounding, honking laugh.

"Enough!" cried Lord Henry. He turned to Polly. "Everyone in the gang gets along, I say. Otherwise, they're out."

Polly pouted unhappily. She glanced at Jack—

this time not a look of hatred but one that wondered if maybe they should be friends.

"What 'as you shot?" Dirty Dick asked Jack.

Jack shook his head. "Nothing."

"What use is that?" complained Bernard.

Lord Henry explained. "These two are my guests. They'll stay by us but not appear. They are not taking part in any holdup—that's a man's job. But we need their help to hide the booty. Jack and Polly are very important to the plan—so all of you hold your tongues, and be polite to my little guests."

The men looked at each other and after a few grumpy looks and some shrugging, they appeared to come to a kind of unspoken agreement. *You wouldn't want to meet these guys on a dark night*, Jack thought, and he smiled at the irony. The dark gray clouds made the afternoon feel like dusk.

"Now," Lord Henry resumed his merry speech, "I have been told by a good friend that the Duke of Belvoir's carriage is to pass on the north road. It'll be packed with rich passengers. But, lads," he cried in a rousing, theatrical voice that made Jack smile, "it is a lonely road, and it is a long and tiresome journey, and I do feel *sorry* for the passengers!"

"Maybe they could do with a little light relief?"

suggested Tom Drum, fixing his mask over his eyes.

"Aye, an encounter with a famous highwayman or two should do the trick!" laughed Pete the Pudding, as if he had just had an idea. "It might pass the time on such a boring journey."

"An' we could make the coach a little lighter— by relieving it of some of those bits of yellow metal an' pretty stones!" Bernard chimed in, his voice as low and deep as a well.

The highwaymen laughed. Tom Drum winked at Jack. And suddenly Jack felt so special to be included in their gang that he entirely forgot about the danger and the time and whether he should be doing what he was doing.

"Stand and deliver!
Lord Henry Vane is the name,
Here to rob you once again!"

Red Ruby reared up on her hind legs and snorted dramatically. Lord Henry's eyes twinkled through the slits on his mask. He twirled his pistol in the air and there was a sudden BANG!

"Oops—I'm terribly sorry," he apologized, laughing. "I am a little twitchy on the trigger today. Please do not be frightened. No one shall be hurt. And never mind, for look! What joy—I have another pistol at the ready!" He grinned as he

produced a second pistol from his coat pocket. The coachman eyed Lord Henry with a mixture of fear and disdain.

Now four masked highwaymen rode up and surrounded the coach. Henry Vane walked Red Ruby forward as Tom Drum dismounted, carrying a sack that he opened up as if preparing to fill it.

Hidden in a tree nearby, Jack looked down on the robbery. When Henry Vane went forward to stop the coach, Jack was surprised to find Polly gripping his arm. He could feel her fear and it made him scared too. But they were safe in the tree. Lord Henry had explained that they always treated the victims with respect. People loved being robbed, he had said with a laugh. They had such a jolly tale to tell their friends in society, and their long and tedious journey was, of course, *so* much more thrilling! In gratitude they often gave something to the poor. It was only right, wasn't it, that the poor should benefit from the rich?

But now that Jack saw the robbery taking place in front of his eyes, he knew that it was wrong. And he suspected that Lord Henry Vane knew it was wrong too—otherwise why would he attempt such an elaborate justification?

"Am I right?" Lord Henry called out merrily. "I have robbed this carriage before?"

"Yes, you have," the coachman said wearily. "Twice."

"Oh! What bad luck!" laughed Lord Henry with pleasure. "It's not the Duke of Belvoir *again*, is it?"

"No, sir. I am taking the duke's houseguests back to London. The duke is not here."

"Shame," said Lord Henry. "I have so enjoyed our meetings. Such a pleasant gentleman with, I must say, *exquisite* taste in clothes. Come on, then. Passengers out, one at a time, please, in a nice, orderly fashion. All offerings thankfully received. We take from the rich, we give to the poor!" he sang.

The door of the carriage opened and a well-dressed, portly gentleman stepped out. He held a small bag of coins. Tom Drum stepped forward and took it with a small bow. He dropped it in the sack with a flourish. The highwaymen clapped.

"Thank you very much," said Lord Henry. "Next!"

An elderly woman in a towering gray wig stepped out. Jack could see how she was shaking. She held out a necklace to Tom Drum and looked straight at Henry Vane. "I know your mother, Henry," she said. "You are a very naughty boy and a great disappointment to her."

At first, silence greeted this bombshell, then the highwaymen snorted with laughter. What a hoot! Jack found their laughter infectious, and he smiled too. It was hard to think of the big man as a naughty little boy.

Henry Vane was silent. Robberies were always exciting. He wanted to snicker like crazy—but he wanted to cry at the same time. His mother! This woman knew his dear mother! He decided to ignore the woman. It was *too* upsetting to think about his mother (but how was she?). And in front of the gang too. He must rise above it.

"Next!" he called coldly.

Out of the carriage stepped a young woman. The hood of her cloak obscured her face, but there was a grace in her movements that made the highwaymen fall silent.

"Hellllllloooooooooooo." Lord Henry's voice purred with appreciation. This was more like it.

"Hello, Henry," replied the woman shakily.

Lord Henry Vane flinched. His face fell and his confidence drained away. He knew this voice. In an instant it took him back to his childhood. It pierced his heart and brought a lump to his throat.

"Who—," he began.

The woman reached up and pulled her hood back to reveal a bright, round, honest face, framed in an arc of small, fair curls. Her blue eyes looked directly at the highwayman.

"Dazzling diamonds," breathed Lord Henry.

"Eh?" Dirty Dick peered at the other highwaymen. Jack sensed that something unexpected was happening. He held the branch above him tightly. There was a change in Lord Henry's voice, a surprise and uncertainty.

Polly whispered, "'Oo's that?"

Jack shook his head and strained to hear.

"Lady Marchwell . . .," Lord Henry began and stopped. The gang of highwaymen shifted uneasily on their horses. They had never seen Henry Vane tongue-tied.

"What have you done, Henry?" the young woman cried out passionately. She looked Henry Vane up and down, upset and disgusted. "How have you sunk so low?"

"Well, I—"

"You are a disgrace to your family."

"Well, I—"

"You! Who were once a bright and golden hope!"

"Yes, I—"

"And now you are a criminal! Henry Vane! The people may laugh at your robberies and your witty little rhymes and your gallant manners—but you are no Robin Hood! You steal for yourself. You are a worthless, common thief!" She spat the word out in disgust. "To think that once I loved you!"

"You—?"

One of the highwaymen snickered and another made an "ooooo" noise. Jack watched as the woman leaned forward and spoke something to Lord Henry. He recoiled as if stung by the words.

"Enough!" shouted Tom Drum, swaggering forward in his fine boots. If His Lordship was stuck for words, *he* would take charge! "Hand over your valuables!" he ordered abruptly and shook his sack at her.

Lady Marchwell glared at him. "Here!" she cried, her eyes filling with tears. She began fumbling with her rings. Her hands trembled so much that she could barely pull them off.

"Emily, please." Lord Henry's voice shook with emotion.

"Emily?" whispered Polly.

"Emily—" Henry Vane's voice broke. This was

discourteous . . . ungentlemanly. What a disaster for his reputation! This was his past—he had betrayed his past. How could he explain? "I . . . I never harmed anybody," he said lamely. "And I do give to the poor." He began to dismount.

"Take this!" Lady Marchwell shrieked, barely controlling her anger. "Here. My engagement ring. And know—I care NOT that you have the ring, for on Saturday I shall have a new ring, given at the Church of Saint Stephen by the Honorable Horace Hogg."

"NO!" yelped Lord Henry, for the news that she was to be married took him by surprise. Such surprise, in fact, that he caught his foot in the stirrup and tumbled into the dust with one leg still stuck in the air. "Oh, foul day! Oh, most vile news! Oh, Hogg. Oh, my leg!"

"Are you all right, my lord?" asked Tom Drum, looking on uselessly.

"Not. All right," growled Lord Henry. His dignity was destroyed, forced as he was to speak upside down between the horse's legs. He spat out the grit and dirt and tried to replace his wig and hat. "Let the lady go," he shouted. "Let them all go. I am ruined. Ruined. And stop standing there like a pumpkin. Help me up!"

Chapter Nine
The Retreat

The highwaymen didn't just let the passengers go. They robbed them first. Jack watched from the tree as beside him Polly muttered under her breath, "Oh, no. Oh, no. Oh, dear me." Lord Henry disentangled himself, cursing all the while, and Dirty Dick, Bad-Breath Bernard, and Pete the Pudding took the jewels and the money and the silver shoe buckles from the passengers and rifled through the two trunks strapped to the back of the carriage.

"Go on!" shouted Lord Henry to the driver when at last he had remounted Red Ruby. "Go on!" He brought his hand down hard on the coach horses' flanks. The driver cracked his whip, and the carriage took off.

The back of Lord Henry's hat was dented, his wig was lopsided, and he had a smear of dirt down one side of his face. He turned to the gang.

"What are you looking at?" he demanded.

"Nothing," snorted Pete the Pudding.

But Jack caught a grin cross the face of Pete the Pudding as he turned away, and there was a stifled snort from Dirty Dick. Henry ignored them. He walked Red Ruby toward Jack and Polly. Jack climbed down onto Henry's horse and sat behind the highwayman. He didn't dare say anything. Henry's face was stony and unreachable.

"Follow us to Wittlesham," he ordered flatly. "Tom, you take Polly. We'll meet at Nanny Manners's house and rest up. You can be sure that they will raise the alarm and the soldiers will be abroad soon."

He nudged his horse and they set off down a bank into the dark forest. Jack clung close as the branches brushed past. Occasionally Henry would say "Down" as they came to an overhanging branch, and they ducked down, but otherwise he was silent.

His pride was wounded. The gang had seen him encounter an old friend. For them it had shed light into his dark past—but for Henry it had shed light on his darker present.

After a while they reached a clear path in the forest and Red Ruby began to trot. Jack bounced up and down uncomfortably. It was lucky that he had ridden a few times on vacations. The other members of the gang followed. No one spoke. Jack felt himself relax. The farther they were from the robbery, the safer they must be, he thought. Staring at the gloomy trees passing, Jack wondered who Lady Marchwell was and how Henry Vane knew her. And then he wondered why Henry Vane was a highwayman. If he had once been a gentleman, why was he now robbing other gentlemen? To give to the poor? Henry pretended highway robbery was a big joke, grand and glamorous, but Jack knew it wasn't. It was a desperate, deadly game.

As they crossed a stream in the woods, Red Ruby's hooves made a clattering noise on the stones, and there was a shout ahead. Jack hardly had time to take it in, but Henry Vane wheeled Red Ruby around in an instant and clattered back through the stream. Jack clung on tightly. Tom Drum was just coming toward them.

Lord Henry leaned over and hissed, "Back! Go

back. The soldiers are camped here!"

The highwaymen immediately turned their horses and spurred them back down the path, as behind them more shouts filled the air. At the edge of the forest, the highwaymen found open ground and raced across, their horses' hooves thudding on the earth. They were well ahead now, but this was no time to relax. Behind them they heard the soldiers calling. If they had guessed that it was the highwayman Henry Vane, they'd soon be searching the surrounding villages.

"Let's go around by Gedgrave," suggested Dirty Dick, "and up by the church."

"They'll be crawling all over the place!" objected Bad-Breath Bernard.

"Not yet," said Lord Henry. "There's time to get to Wittlesham."

"And don't you worry yourselves," Tom Drum said with glee. "We've got a hideout in Wittlesham. It's so good you'll never believe it. Trust me—they'll never find us! Not in a hundred years."

They abandoned their horses on the outskirts of the village. Henry left Red Ruby in a farmyard, and the others disappeared down a lane. Jack was relieved to

be off the horse. Then Jack, Polly, and the highwaymen raced past the little thatched cottages into the
old village square. The daylight was fading, dusk
falling around them.

"Mrs. Manners is in the Cap and Stockings with
Old Ma Cracklepot," Polly whispered to Henry.

"Good."

"But the house is no place to hide," she told
them. "The soldiers came the other night. They
searched all the houses. They crawled over us."

"Ah, but we've got a secret," Henry Vane replied,
arching his eyebrow. "Haven't we, Jack?"

"You bet," Jack replied. For a second he worried that the hideout might no longer be there, then he dismissed the thought from his mind.

"Lead on, Jack Bolt," said Lord Henry. A playfulness seemed to be returning and Jack glimpsed the flash of white teeth.

He led them up the rickety stairs into the bedroom. And then to the fireplace. Beside the grate he found the iron plate that was the secret door into his bedroom. At the top he found the clasp and he twisted it. The iron plate fell open toward him and he saw his bedroom on the other side. He smiled. "Come on."

The men crawled through, one after the other. They emerged into Jack's bedroom, a secret room in another time. At once the atmosphere changed. This was a lighter, friendlier world—at least as far as Jack was concerned. He noticed how the streetlight in the square gave a yellowish tinge to the light in the room. He heard a car. He heard the beep of an electronic lock. How strangely reassuring they were. He looked around at the big shapes of the men filling the room.

They were speaking to each other softly:

" 'Tis not natural."

"I is right and proper spooked."

". . . like entering a new world."

"'Tis the spell of a witch . . ."

"'Tis a holy deliverance!"

"Are we all here? Good." Lord Henry closed the hole in the wall.

Everyone breathed easily again. Then they gathered around the window and peered in disbelief at the transformation that had taken place in the humble village.

"Jack! Jack! Is that you?" It was Granny calling from downstairs.

"Yes, Granny!"

"At last! Please will you come down? It's suppertime. I've been calling for ages."

"I'm coming!"

Jack hastily explained to the highwaymen that this was his granny's house. They had to be quiet and not move around and not make a sound. Then, changing out of the rough clothes, he pulled on his sweater and jeans and went downstairs.

Chapter Ten
Burglars

The morning dawned crisp and clear. There was a red sky in the east and the autumn leaves hung in the trees like golden coins.

Jack opened his eyes. The previous night's events hit him like a bolt from the blue. He sat up in bed.

BOING!

Oh, Granny. His bones ached. He stared around the room. There were footprints across the carpet. There were black marks on the wall. The chair was broken; the curtain hung like a flag at half-mast. The chest had been moved and there were blankets and clothes and black cloaks slung around the place. There was a cheesy, rancid smell of feet and wood smoke. But there were no highwaymen. The highwaymen had gone.

At first Jack felt a curious mixture of relief and sadness. The five highwaymen and the girl from another time had bedded down here for the night. It was like a sleepover, except instead of his friends he had a gang of highwaymen. After they had asked Jack a million questions about the modern world, and he told them about cars and TVs and telephones and computers and streetlights and history and clothes and toothbrushes and even things like dinosaurs and planets that they had never heard of, they relaxed and became accustomed to the idea that they had traveled forward into another time. Then they told stories and cracked funny jokes and laughed in a low, gruff way.

Soon after they had settled, Polly pointed out that they should block the hole in the wall, in case the soldiers found it. So they moved the chest until it was covering the hole. Later, the soldiers did come—and they found the secret cupboard door, but when they looked in all they saw was the inside of a chest. Little did they know that on the other side, five highwaymen were sitting in nervous silence.

Jack smiled. That was a cool moment. Outwitting

the soldiers had been fun. Outwitting Granny had been more difficult. She hadn't looked as if she believed him for an instant when he told her he had been out for a walk for most of yesterday. Then he told her he had been listening to music on his headphones upstairs and hadn't heard her call. She had given him that beady bird stare, the one that went right through him.

But Jack's relief changed to concern when he wondered where the highwaymen and Polly had gone. He assumed they had gone back to the eighteenth century, maybe to do another robbery, or to have breakfast. Jack decided he would go and look for them after his own breakfast. He was hungry.

As he went downstairs, he was startled by a cry. He found Granny by the front door, hands on hips, staring at the wall.

"Would you believe it!" she exclaimed. "It's gone! The clock. Someone's stolen the clock!" She glanced around. "And my big magnifying glass!" She turned to Jack. "I came down and the door was open. And these things have gone. Look! The pens! All the pens and pencils in the pencil pot have gone! You haven't seen them, have you?"

Jack shook his head. He tried not to blush, not to look guilty. He kept his mouth shut tight, but the words came unbidden into his head. "I know who stole them. Some highwaymen from the eighteenth century. They came for a sleepover . . ." But he said nothing.

"Humph." Granny began blinking. It was a habit of hers and made her look even more birdlike. "Something fishy is going on here," she mumbled.

"Yeah," agreed Jack.

Twenty minutes later, in the middle of breakfast, the answer came. Jack was sitting at the table eating toast when Granny let out a squeal of surprise.

"Good grief! What on earth are *those?*"

Jack looked up to see five dark figures crossing the square. They wore cloaks and hats and had a little peasant girl with them. They looked so out of place. Why, oh why couldn't they have stayed in his room?

"I—"

"They're looking at our house!" said Granny suspiciously. The men were pointing up at the windows and talking energetically. "Are they some sort of pop cult?"

"I—"

"Look, they're waving! Do you know them?" Granny turned to Jack. Tom Drum was pointing and waving at Jack. He had a stupid expression on his face.

Jack waved back.

"I've never seen them before." Then he added quietly, "In the square." Behind his granny's back, he changed his wave to say "go away." And he made a face at Lord Henry. Luckily Polly began pulling the other highwaymen away.

Then before Jack could stop her, Granny opened the back door and called out to the men. "Do we know you?" and without waiting for an answer she went on, "I know it is Halloween, but I've never seen anyone dressed up so early in the day."

"Indeed, ma'am," said one of the men. "Good day to you!" He doffed his hat and ushered the men away to the far end of the square by the churchyard.

"Most peculiar," sighed Granny. "What do you say nowadays? Weirdos. I've half a mind to call the police. Without the slightest proof, I'd say they looked like burglars!"

"Burglars?" Jack ate his toast very fast. "Hmm. I suppose they do look kind of like that."

Chapter Eleven
All Hallows' Eve

"What's going on? What are you doing?" Jack caught up with the highwaymen in the churchyard. They were hanging around the gravestones, stooped over like big black birds, reading the inscriptions.

"We are concealing ourselves from the soldiers. In the twenty-first century." Henry Vane turned on his irresistible smile. "We must wait till darkness before we return to our time, for then the soldiers will be away. And while we are waiting, we thought we would have a little look around. Like you, we desire to see what life is like here."

"And who stole the clock and the magnifying

glass and pencils?" Jack demanded.

Henry Vane frowned. He looked quizzically at the other men.

"Er, I found the clock," admitted Bernard, sheepishly producing the hall clock from his cloak.

"And I saw these—they is so pretty," said Pete the Pudding. He pulled out a handful of pens and pencils. "And Dick took a liking to the magic glass, which makes things seem wondrous big."

"Well—give them back!" Jack told them firmly. "I'll get into trouble. They belong to Granny."

Henry Vane shook his head. "We abuse our friend's hospitality here—indeed we do! No swiping or filching or taking a liking to things from now on. Is that clear?"

The men nodded.

"Nor no robbin'?" asked Tom Drum. "Not even a little highway robbin'?"

"Certainly not. How can we rob without horses?" Henry frowned. His attention was suddenly riveted to a man in a yellow and black striped running suit jogging past the graveyard.

"The man is like a vast bumblebee," he observed. Jack could tell the highwaymen were in for some surprises here in the twenty-first century.

"The problem is," said Dirty Dick, "the people here are all dressed funny. All colorful, like a carnival. We stick out, you know. Like sober people at some revelry."

"Has it occurred to you," asked Polly, "that it's not *them* who is dressed funny—it's *you*!"

Dirty Dick scowled.

"Maybe it doesn't matter," Jack told them, "because tonight is Halloween. Everyone dresses up as ghosts and vampires and scary things. So if you meet people you could say 'Happy Halloween—we've dressed up as scary highwaymen.' And they won't care that you're dressed strangely."

"Ghosts and vampires?" repeated Dirty Dick. "What a strange thing to do."

"Oh! Halloween is like our All Hallows' Eve, then?" said Pete the Pudding.

"Of course," said Polly, "it must be."

"So, in the twenty-first century, everyone knows about highwaymen?" asked Lord Henry. His interest was aroused, his eyebrow arched.

"Sure. Everyone knows Dick Turpin," Jack told him.

"Dick Turpin?" Lord Henry was outraged. His eyes bulged and his lip curled. "*Dick Turpin!* Why do they remember Dick Turpin?"

"I don't know."

"He's a rascal. A common criminal. No style, no breeding, not an ounce of gallantry in him! Why *him*?" he spluttered and sat down on a gravestone like a sulky boy.

Jack was surprised. "He's just famous, I guess."

"And I'm not? No one remembers Lord Henry Vane? And the Vane Gang—of course?"

"Well. No. I guess not."

"Oh!" Henry Vane couldn't conceal his disappointment. He turned his back. His dreams of fame had evaporated in a cruel instant.

Polly nudged Jack and rolled her eyes as if to say, "This isn't the behavior of a heroic highwayman." Jack smiled. Polly couldn't care less about fame.

"I'm starving," she said. "I haven't eaten for hours."

"Me too," said Pete the Pudding. "Where can we get a handsome breakfast around here? I could eat a couple of sheep."

"Well, I can't get you any sheep, but"—Jack remembered that his mom had given him some emergency money—"I'll get something from the supermarket."

"A super breakfast from the super market," sang Tom Drum cheerfully.

★ ★ ★

Jack ran back to the house with the clock and the pencils and the magnifying glass. He put them on the floor, trying to make it look as if they had accidentally fallen off the wall and the desk. He ran up to his ruined bedroom and found his emergency money. Then he ran over to the small supermarket, where he bought cookies, cold pies, sandwiches, and some Halloween ghostie chocolate bars.

As he left the supermarket, he caught sight of a figure dressed in a cloak and hat emerging from the antique shop on the other side of the square. It was Dirty Dick. Jack hurried to the graveyard.

"I did it!" Dick was explaining excitedly to the others. His eyes were lit up and he was grinning foolishly. "New money for old! I gave the shop-keeper—an 'antique' dealer—a shilling and he gave me seventy-five new pounds! That is a fair exchange, eh, lads? And look—there's a queen on the throne: Elizabeth the Second. Here." He generously handed out the notes. The others crowded around to examine them.

"Did he question your garments?" asked Lord Henry. Jack noticed that the highwaymen were growing fascinated by the ways of this new world. How long would it take for them to feel completely at home? And if they did, what then?

"Aye, so he did—but wait for it—*he* was dressed in some light jacket of a violent blue, with breeches that clung to his skin. A meaner cut I never did see—his tailor kept an abundance of cloth for himself, I do reckon. And what a sunlit emporium! Light! Like you are surrounded by a firmament of dazzling stars! I could see every pore on his pearly skin!"

"What did he say about your clothes?" asked Jack.

"He said for a moment he was frightened I was going to hold up the shop! Ha! And I said that would be a merry prank! Then I took out my pistols, and he turned pale and wished that he could vanish forthwith. I said that he looked like a ghost—so we were both well dressed for Halloween! And then we had a laugh and I put away the pistols and we exchanged the money."

Jack felt queasy. He suddenly realized that he felt responsible for the highwaymen. He hadn't thought that they would be walking around the village with pistols. Surely that was against the law? He was about to say as much when he found a little hand wriggling against his chest, tugging at the food. He turned to find Polly. "Can I have some?" she asked.

"Sure."

A cry went up when they saw she was eating a pie, for they all wanted one. Jack watched as they tore into the pies and sandwiches. It looked as if they hadn't been fed for weeks. Two of them began eating the plastic, not realizing that it had to be removed first.

"Chewy," said Bernard.

"An' not very tasty," declared Pete.

"It's plastic," Jack laughed. "You're not supposed to eat that."

The highwaymen judged each piece of food in this new age. The pastry, they thought, was like parchment and would be good for writing a letter on but was lousy for eating.

The meat and gravy were good, though (beggin'

your pardon, Jack), it was a tiny portion that would hardly satisfy an ant.

Chips were nice and salty, though like eating air—"Nothing to get yer teeth into," complained Tom Drum.

But the cookies: sweet and delicious! They chomped through two bags in a minute and a half. Then they each had the ghostie chocolate bar.

"Booootiful. Georgeous. Tummy-tingling," they said. They had never tasted chocolate in this form before—in their time chocolate was only a drink and never so sweet.

Jack found himself laughing at them all. They were like children just entering a theme park—giggling excitedly at the bright new world before them. Only Henry was distracted. He lingered by the yew tree a little way off, deep in thought. When he noticed Jack watching him, he straightened his back and seemed to throw off the thoughts that had been weighing him down.

"Come on, everyone, I think it is time for us to explore the town. This is a small town, and it will be a good way to spend the day."

Jack looked at the ragged bunch of ruffians. He wasn't sure that it *was* a good way to spend the day.

Chapter Twelve
Snippers of Wittlesham

So that they attracted less attention, the highway-men split up into three groups and set off. Jack took Henry and Polly to the main street. Henry's mood lifted, and he behaved as if he was on vacation. He laughed and joked, and as they walked out of the churchyard and down the old lane to the main street, he doffed his hat to passers-by and behaved with excessive courtesy—until Jack pointed out that this was drawing unwanted attention to themselves.

"I was only being polite," he said.

In the main street, Henry admired the ready-made clothes, the violin-maker, and the bookstore. "A very cultured place is Wittlesham now, for sure."

They examined the fruit and vegetable stand, the liquor store, the grocery store, and an Indian restaurant. "There is so much food!" Polly marveled. "Why has no one eaten it? And how strangely it is stored! In jars and boxes and soft glass!"

"That's plastic," Jack told them. "And those things are metal cans," he explained.

"Truly this is a land of plenty," said Henry, smiling.

And then they came to the hairdresser's: Snippers of Wittlesham.

Lord Henry's eyes lit up. He purred. "I am in desperate need of a coiff," he declared, and before Jack or Polly could stop him, he had walked in and was greeting the receptionist.

"Good day to you, madam!" He bowed low. Jack and Polly hovered uneasily by the door.

"Have you known him long?" whispered Jack. He wanted to get to know Polly better, but talking to her with all the grown-up highwaymen around wasn't easy.

"All me life," Polly answered him. "Since when I lost Ma. He is grand. And kind. But sometimes—Nanny Manners says—he is as stupid and stubborn as a mule. She says he needs looking after."

Jack watched as Lord Henry charmed the

receptionist, who had decided to join in the fun.

"Good day, sire!" she laughed. "What can I do you for this merry Halloween?"

Henry beamed. "First, Mistress Snippers: a cut. Then a shave. Then I would have you dry and set this. I must look my best." Taking off his hat, he whipped off his enormous wig. Underneath, he had disappointingly straight and straggly hair. " 'Tis somewhat soggy, due to the abundance of rain last week."

The lady whooped when she saw the wig and called out to her friend. "Martha! We got Dick Turpin here; requires some attention."

"I'm not Dick Turpin. I'm Lord Henry Vane," Lord Henry informed her pompously.

The lady whooped again. "It's Lord Henry, Martha! Cut and blow-dry and some wig maintenance! We don't do shaves." She grabbed the wig and threw it to Martha, who had been sitting hunched over some magazines.

"Sleep in a hedge last night?" she asked as she washed his hair.

"Certainly not," he replied.

"Them clothes are just perfect!" the hairdresser told Henry as she began cutting.

"I know," Lord Henry purred. "The coat is

particularly fine. Silk from the Indies and a lining of chinoiserie. Very à la mode."

"Ohhh, you won't stop pretending, will you?" she said. "What's your real job, then? Eh? When you're not being a Halloween highwayman."

"Nothing, madam."

"Oooo. Must be an actor, then! Ha, ha!" She had a baying nasal laugh. Jack and Polly exchanged a look. The hairdresser was just as odd as Lord Henry. Suddenly she turned on the blow-dryer and began blasting Henry with hot air. He leaped out of his chair.

"Mistress Snippers!" he exclaimed. "What in the king's name are you doing?"

"It's a blow-dry, love, now calm down!" She was beginning to think this client was behaving oddly. It surely wasn't necessary to keep up the pretense of being a highwayman *all* the time. It was just plain weird.

In a few minutes, after Lord Henry had relaxed, she said, "All done."

"More of the blow-dry, please." Henry's eyes were closed in pleasure.

"It's dry, darling—you don't need any more."

"But I like it."

Martha appeared with the wig. She held it at

arm's length. "I dried it off," she said, "but it's gross. You wouldn't catch me wearing it."

"Your meaning, madam?" inquired Lord Henry.

"It stinks. It's like a hairy cheese."

"It is the finest set of curls available. From Perkins and Chase in Bond Street, no less." He stuffed the wig into a large inside pocket of his coat.

"That's twenty pounds, please," said Mistress Snippers.

"Twenty pounds!" spluttered Lord Henry. "I could buy a house for that!"

"Not around here you couldn't!" She laughed. "'Bye, Lord Henry. Happy Halloween."

He paid her the money. Relieved to have Lord Henry back before the hairdressers became more suspicious, Jack and Polly each took an arm and escorted him out.

"Where to now?" asked Lord Henry, admiring his new haircut in the reflection of a shop window. His hair was clean and clipped and glossy. His spirits were high. "This suits my plan very well," he declared. "To look my most appealing."

Ahead of them were two suspicious-looking characters in cloaks and hats. Dirty Dick and Pete the Pudding were looking in a store window.

The sign above read WILCOX AND CO. JEWELERS. Jack, Polly, and Lord Henry arrived just in time to hear Dick say darkly, "Are you thinking what I'm thinking?"

In the store window before them lay a carpet of glittering stones, rings, watches, necklaces, and bracelets, all sparkling with tiny diamonds and rubies and sapphires. Treasure, only inches from their eyes. It was too tantalizing.

"NO," said Jack firmly.

The men spun around. "Look, Henry! Feast yer eyes upon it! They is little jewels, to be sure, but what a lot of them! We could have them and in a bound be back in the old Wittlesham."

"It certainly is a tempting sight," said Lord Henry. He sighed. His eyes twinkled, as if caught in a trance.

"Come *on*," said Jack, dragging them away.

In the street, people were looking at the highwaymen, sometimes laughing and smiling, sometimes just staring. As shoppers passed by, they made comments: "How'ye do?" "Look out—it's the caped crusaders," "Stand and deliver, my son!"—even "Bless you, Your Holiness," from an elderly woman.

Jack thanked his lucky stars it was Halloween.

After a while they reached the edge of the town, where they could look across the fields, toward the hills. Lord Henry was surprised to see how bare it was. The fields were huge—twenty times as big as any he had ever seen—and in the distance, electricity poles marched in a line across the horizon. So many trees had gone.

Jack felt Lord Henry's mood become reflective. He was quiet for some time, gazing out. "How it has changed," he said, gently now. "When I was growing up, England was covered in trees. From Vane Park we could walk for two days to within sight of the spires of London and never leave the forest."

"Is that where you live now?" asked Jack.

"No, Jack. I was brought up in the mansion, but I left it when I was twenty-one. Ah, me. I had money and I spent it. And when it is gone, it is gone." He let out a great and heartfelt sigh.

"Couldn't you earn some more?" asked Jack.

"Earn?" Lord Henry looked bewildered, as if the idea of earning money was hard to grasp. He pulled his cloak around him. "Dear me, no. No, no. My mother would have bequeathed me more. Only my father was dead. And my elder brother refused me.

He said I frittered it away on cards and dinners and loose living. But I *had* to have money because I owed it. I had borrowed so much. So I robbed. Only a little here and there, from those who have plenty. And I have never hurt a hair—never a hair—on their heads."

"And your friend Lady Marchwell?" asked Jack.

Lord Henry looked down at his boots. His eyebrows knitted together. Jack knew he had touched on a sensitive subject.

"Ah. Emily Marchwell. She lived near Vane Park. A pretty child, whom I met at dances and country

balls. I loved her from afar. Yet I never told her. I always thought she was too, too good. I never knew she loved me. I never thought for an instant that she would. Until . . . until yesterday." He sighed and spoke as if it was painful. "Yesterday she said that it was me whom she loved. And she might still if . . . if it wasn't for the Honorable Hogg . . ." He winced as he spoke the name.

"Who is he?" asked Jack gently.

Lord Henry scowled. "An ancient old walnut of a man! Dried and wrinkled and wizened with age. And warty withal. She can only be marrying him to please her father. For he is rich, and she will be his trophy." He trembled with anger.

"Lady Marchwell did seem kind and true to me," said Polly, shooting a worried glance at Jack.

"Aye, well, so she did. But he? Hogg! Oh! He is a scheming man, a dry stick of a man . . . You know I felt her first warmth, like the sun on the cold earth, bringing me to life, as forth a flower . . ."

Jack struggled to make sense of Lord Henry's speech. The man seemed in turmoil, tortured by doubts, confused by passion.

". . . in fact, I do believe a little love is still reserved for me," Lord Henry declared at length, "and maybe she might love me still and . . . and . . . I might love her. Yes! If only I had seized my chance! For it is all in the timing . . . Instead, I . . . I, oh, dear! But what can I do?"

Jack stared into the distance. He didn't know what to suggest. He glanced over at Polly. She looked alarmed, as if she had never seen a man behave like this.

"Well," Jack began, thinking that love, like other difficulties, should be dealt with in as straight-forward a way as possible. "Maybe if you told her, you know, she'd understand?"

Lord Henry put his hand on Jack's shoulder. He turned his dark eyes on the boy and looked at him intensely. For a moment Jack wondered if he had said something wrong. Henry's eyes were mournful, like a puppy's. Jack knew people agonized over love, but he couldn't understand why. Lord Henry smiled ruefully. "Maybe she would understand or maybe she would turn me in and send me to the gallows. How forgiving is her heart, Jack?"

"Er, I don't know," Jack admitted and just stopped himself from shrugging. "Probably quite forgiving?" he suggested, feeling out of his depth.

Chapter Thirteen
The Halloween Highwaymen

Jack went back to Granny's for lunch, leaving the highwaymen to go to the Cap and Stockings. Now that they had some money, they could afford a good lunch. And as long as they were at the pub, Jack felt, they couldn't get into too much trouble. Could they?

Granny had found the clock, the magnifying glass, and the pencils and declared herself puzzled.

"Must've fallen down," Jack suggested.

"Hmm," Granny wondered. "Very peculiar," she said ominously.

Granny then told Jack that she was sorry, but she would be busy at a village committee meeting later in the afternoon, and it was bound to run long, so she had prepared supper and put it in the fridge in case he got hungry.

"Why don't you go trick-or-treating with the Price children?" she suggested.

Jack winced. The Prices? The computer geeks? They probably did virtual trick-or-treating on their computers. He would rather swim the English Channel. In the winter. With sharks.

"Um, maybe," he said vaguely.

"What? Should I call Mrs. Price?"

"No! Please. I'll go and see them myself," he told Granny loudly.

When lunch was finished, Jack went upstairs to his wrecked bedroom and watched the entrance to the Cap and Stockings pub. He had no intention of going trick-or-treating with the Price children. He'd tell Granny that he had called but there was no answer. "Price?" he called softly. There was no answer. *One less lie to account for*, he thought to himself.

The highwaymen spent all afternoon in the Cap and Stockings. From up in his bedroom Jack could look down on the pub, but he could see only their breeches and black boots appearing every now and then. What were they doing? How long would they be? Surely the other customers would find out who they really were? And what then?

To his surprise, Jack found that he now felt quite protective of them. They were his friends and he wanted them for himself. He didn't want to share this adventure. If he told someone—anyone—and they believed him, then they were bound to take the adventure away from him.

Now he wanted to get the highwaymen back to their own time, before anything went wrong. Imagine what the newspapers and TV would do if they found out. They'd go into a frenzy. Imagine the cameras and people who would surround his bedroom for the chance to quiz highwaymen from the eighteenth century. It would probably give Granny a heart attack.

As Jack sat at the window, color slowly drained out of the world and the low sun slipped over the horizon. There was a brief, spectacular sunset. Still no one came out of the Cap and Stockings. Inside, the lights were turned on and a warm and inviting glow beckoned in the gathering dusk.

What were they doing in there?

At last Polly appeared. Her rough peasant clothes looked so out of place. She glanced up at Jack's bedroom window and saw him. She motioned with a quick nod of her head, and he ran down to meet her.

"They're all playing cards," she told him, walking toward the churchyard. The trees were silhouetted black against the palest yellow sky. Polly was angry. "They're gambling. You know: win money, lose money, fight. I don't like it. It's stupid."

"They fight?" asked Jack, alarmed.

"Yeah. They usually fight. 'Cause someone always cheats. They can't stop themselves cheating. It's in their highwayman blood!"

"Is that what you want to be, Polly? A highwayman?" Jack asked. He put his foot on a wooden post and climbed up onto the church wall.

Polly scowled. "Highway*woman*," she corrected him. She sat next to him on the wall, looking quite fierce and dangling her legs. "I did. But I ain't so sure now. Seems that whatever I do, it ain't good enough. I capture you—'cause I thought you was a thief—and they laugh. I ride with them and help save them from the soldiers and he won't even let me have a drink."

"But why do you want to be a highwaywoman?"

Polly looked at Jack. People were pretty nosy in this century. "Lord Henry. I suppose he is like my father. I never knew my father—but Henry is like what he would be. If you see what I mean."

"But if you are caught, wouldn't you be hanged?" asked Jack.

Polly nodded. "Yeah. But maybe I could do it for a bit and then stop?"

"I suppose so," said Jack, struggling to see the sense in it at all.

"Yeah, well. I could pick potatoes and churn butter all me life. *If I'm lucky!*" she said.

Jack was quiet. How could he hope to understand someone from another century? One thing he did know—he was glad to be born now, in the twenty-first century.

In the window of a house nearby, a jack-o'-lantern appeared, its grinning face scaring away spirits while attracting children. Jack explained what it was. Polly liked the idea of scaring spirits on a dark night. Soon the children came, silhouettes in the gloom, dressed up as pale ghosts, bloodthirsty vampires, ghastly ghouls, or witches. They didn't come into the graveyard. They went with their flashlights down the darkening street, ringing doorbells, knocking on doors, and squealing with delight.

"They don't believe in witches, do they?" asked Polly.

"No." Jack didn't want to know then that witches were real.

"Us here—that is witchcraft," said Polly, almost to herself.

"Yes," Jack agreed. It had to be.

"I'm sorry I tied you up," she said, turning to look at him. She was so friendly now. "I didn't know all this was here."

"That's all right."

"I want to go back," she said, shivering. "I don't belong here. None of us does."

Their conversation was cut short by the eruption

of the highwaymen from the Cap and Stockings. They came out, laughing and talking in loud voices.

"Over here!" Polly called, waving in the dark.

"Hey, Polly, look at this." Tom Drum showed her a postcard of Wittlesham. He struck a match so that she could see it.

"Look. You can see every tile on the roof, every blade of grass. A miracle."

"It's a photograph," said Jack.

"What's that?" Tom Drum was baffled.

Jack explained.

"Marvelous," the highwaymen declared. "That's progress. The things we will learn."

A little masked child came around the corner. "Stick 'em up!" he cried.

"OOOO, I am frightened," said Bernard in his deep, rumbling voice.

"Come here, Martin," said the child's mother when she saw Bernard's scar.

"An' look," said Dirty Dick when the mother and child had disappeared around the corner, "I got this!" He opened his hand to show a neat black wallet. "Hee hee—I swiped it from that card player in the pub! What a dolt! I cheated him good and proper!"

"You numskull," growled Lord Henry. "You horse-headed loon! What did you do that for?"

"Evening, lads," said a voice. A beam of light pierced through the darkness and lit up their faces. "A bit old for trick-or-treating, aren't we?"

Jack's heart jumped. *Police!*

"You're never too old," Jack said, bravely taking charge. "They got dressed up for me."

"Only you *haven't* dressed up?" observed the policeman, picking out Jack with his flashlight.

There was a shuffling as Dirty Dick hid the wallet he had stolen.

"Stand and deliver!" said Tom Drum playfully. He stuck out his fingers to make a pistol.

"I am from the Hertfordshire Constabulary," said the man. "Police Constable Manners is the name— so watch your Ps and Qs!" he warned them merrily.

"Constable!" spluttered Dirty Dick.

A shiver of nervousness ran through the highwaymen, and they huddled together.

"Just keeping an eye out on a night like this . . . Lots of terrible crimes in the air, you know." His flashlight played across their faces. "Crikey! You lot look like the real McCoy: where did you get the costumes and the makeup?"

"I've got a costume box," explained Jack. He couldn't believe he was telling such a paper-thin lie.

"Oh, well—don't hold up any coaches or I'll be after you!" laughed the policeman. "You are clearly very wicked men! And boys and girls. Ha, ha! Happy Halloween!"

He stalked off into the night, whistling.

"Happy Halloween!" the highwaymen chorused as sweetly as they were able (which was pretty murderously).

"That was close," breathed Dirty Dick.

But before anyone could agree, there was a shout from the Cap and Stockings and a man ran out of the pub.

"They've stolen my wallet, the thieving sots!" he cried. "Hey!" he shouted to the police constable. "I've just been robbed! They've stolen my wallet. It's got my credit cards and a wad of cash."

They watched with mounting alarm as the policeman walked over to the Cap and Stockings and began talking to the man.

"Time to go," declared Lord Henry coolly.

They took off like a flock of blackbirds into the night—boots pounding the pavement, cloaks flapping behind them. Polly and Jack were in the thick of it, friends now, as they both had an interest in the highwaymen. They charged through the church-yard, out of the far entrance, to an alley behind. They flew along the alley, swooping around the corner to approach the square from another direction.

Sneakily, suspiciously, they tiptoed into Granny Bolt's house and bounded up to Jack's room. Jack was thankful Granny was still out. From the bed-room they could look down at the constable. He was below them, speaking on his radio. A moment later he walked briskly over to the churchyard gates.

It was clear on whom he had pinned this particular crime.

"Let's go back," said Lord Henry. "Not a minute to lose."

He picked up Dirty Dick's hat. His hands were shaking. "Now we're wanted in *both* places, you bearded buffoon!" He whacked Dirty Dick with the hat.

"Sorry, my lord," said Dirty Dick.

Lord Henry turned to Jack. "That constable will want to talk to you too," he said.

"I know." Even though Jack hadn't stolen the wallet, he was involved with the highwaymen, and

the policeman had seen Jack with them. Now Jack would have to lie low. And if the highwaymen could hide in his time, why couldn't he hide in the highwaymen's time?

"Can I come with you?" Jack asked.

Henry Vane smiled. "It is my most fervent wish. It is the perfect solution! For in my time, I believe the soldiers will now be gone, and we shall have safe passage through the darkness." He put his arm around Jack's shoulder and drew him aside. "Jack, I have a favor to ask of you." He spoke in a warm, rich voice. Jack looked up into Lord Henry's eyes: their friendliness made him feel almost dizzy. "Will you come to London and help me win Lady

Marchwell's hand?" he asked.

"Well, I—"

"Think about it," said the highwayman hopefully.

They were interrupted by a cry. "What do we do about this purse? The one Dirty Dick has stolen—*against the rules.*" Pete the Pudding waved the wallet in the air.

"Keep it," said a grinning Bernard, and he shrugged.

"Bah! That money is no good in our time," said Dirty Dick, now wishing he hadn't taken it.

"Why don't we throw it out of the window onto the road?" suggested Polly.

"Now *that* is an especially good idea!" declared Pete the Pudding in admiration.

Bernard scratched his head and looked uncertain.

Polly beamed. "Make it look as if the man dropped it. Look, you can see the Cap and Stockings from here." She opened the window that looked down on the pub. "Just throw it out and then someone'll find it and think the man made a mistake."

Before they left, Jack ran downstairs. He needed to let Granny know he was okay—or at least try to

110

keep her from worrying. What with keeping the highwaymen on track, stopping them getting into trouble, preventing anybody finding out about who they really were, and making sure that Granny wasn't worried about him and wouldn't miss him— he felt like his brain would explode. Life was getting seriously complicated!

He quickly wrote out a note for Granny saying that he had had supper and gone to bed. Then he went back upstairs and stuffed some pillows under his sheets. He put on the smock and rough sacking trousers over his jeans. Then he locked the room on the inside.

"I'm ready," he said.

The highwaymen quietly removed the chest covering the hole into the eighteenth century.

"Let's go."

Chapter Fourteen
Naughty Boy

It was dark, like a cellar at midnight. The high-waymen shuffled into the room bumping into each other. Jack could smell the pigs.

"Where's the door?" whispered Pete the Pudding.

"Here," said Bernard. There was a crumbling noise of plaster falling onto floorboards. "Ah. Sorry. It's the curtain."

Jack snickered.

"He's ripped the curtains down!" exclaimed Tom Drum, as the faintest glimmer of starlight came through the tiny window.

"Hush!" said Lord Henry, crawling through and

shutting the metal plate to Jack's room.

"I've found the door," said Polly. "Stay here—the soldiers may be downstairs."

"If there are any soldiers downstairs, then they'll know we're here. Unless they think a herd of cattle has stumbled through the roof," said Pete, rubbing his head.

"Flying cattle," joked Jack.

"Oi! You just poked me in the eye!" complained Dirty Dick.

"Come down this minute," said a sharp voice from downstairs. "Henry Arthur Vane! NOW!"

The highwaymen fell silent.

"Oh, dear," said Lord Henry. "Nanny Manners. Now I'm in for it."

"You naughty boy," said Tom Drum, grinning.

"All of you!" Nanny Manners demanded fiercely.

They trooped down the rickety staircase into the kitchen. There was an oil lamp burning on the table and candles in the window. Nanny Manners stood in front of the fire with her arms folded and a furious look on her face. She reminded Jack of his principal. Except Nanny Manners wielded a wooden spoon.

"Is this how you return my kindness, Henry?" she

demanded. "I offer you a safe house—my own house, my own secrets—and you bring this ragtag bunch of do-nothings and criminals in for fun?"

"Nanny, these are good gentlemen."

"Good gentlemen? Fiddle faddle! They are highwaymen! Land pirates! They'd slit your throat as soon as look at you! And these two innocents: Polly here, an orphan—and the boy! Look at him! Young colt!"

"He's a fine fellow—"

"He may be! But *you* are not."

"Nanny," Lord Henry murmured in a soothing voice. He put his hands out to plead with her, and he flashed his charming smile.

Whack! Nanny Manners nimbly stepped forward and rapped his hands with the wooden spoon. She wasn't taken in.

"Ow!"

"I've had soldiers crawling all over this place, with their dirty feet and their rude ways," she screeched. "Someone's tipped them off that you're here. You have been this close to swinging on the silken rope, my boy. You don't know how lucky you are. It's time you mended your ways."

"Nanny—"

"OUT!" she cried. "I've said my piece, and I want you all OUT."

"But the soldiers may find us—"

"NOW!" She pointed her trembling wooden spoon to the door. They began the slow, inevitable shuffle, heads hanging.

"I'm sorry, Nanny," whispered Lord Henry as he left.

"OUT!" Nanny Manners threw her wooden spoon in frustration after them. It clattered to the floor.

Jack was the last to leave. The old woman stared at him. "Be careful, boy," he thought he heard her say. "You don't have long."

Jack slipped out as fast as he could. Nanny Manners was spooky.

Outside it was cool. The sky was clear and the moon was just coming up above the trees. Lights in the one or two cottages showed dimly. The pigs grunted. A dog barked.

"You naughty boy," said Dirty Dick, grinning like an idiot.

"Shut up," said Lord Henry.

"Is this how you return my kindness, Henry?" mimicked Pete with a snort.

"She is the only person in the land who can talk to me like that," said Henry tersely.

"She still loves you," Tom Drum consoled him. "Always will."

"So?" asked Bernard, giving himself a good scratch. "Now what?"

"We fetch the horses and go," snapped Lord Henry, trying to reassert his authority. "I have business in London. Something I should have done years ago. And London is as good as the forest for us to hide in. The soldiers and constables will never find us there. Will you come?"

"Well, there's nothing for us here," said Dirty Dick. "London's the place to be."

"What about the boy?" asked Tom Drum.

"And the girl? Don't forget I'm one of the gang now," Polly reminded them.

"No, Polly," said Lord Henry. "Please."

"You said I was," Polly said indignantly. "And I heard you are a man of your word."

"Very well." Lord Henry sighed. He didn't have the stomach for a fight with Polly. "Have you a horse?"

"I can get one," Polly said.

"Then fetch it. And get Jack some clothes. We'll

meet by Wagoners Lane." Henry swept his cloak over his shoulders. "You'll come, Jack?" he asked kindly.

"Okay," Jack told him.

"Splendid. We'll pick up a horse for you on the way."

Lord Henry took Jack by the arm and set off. He strode away, around the house and up the dark street.

"Wait." Jack pulled away from Lord Henry and looked back at the house. He could just make out its shape in the moonlight. It was so different from Granny Bolt's house. For a start, it was thatched. It was smaller too: a humble cottage with one room downstairs and two little bedrooms upstairs. Next to the cottage was a low shed: the pigsty. And above the pigsty: nothing. Thin air. In time—how much time he wasn't sure—his bedroom would be there.

"Come on," said Henry, tugging his arm.

They walked up the street, through wood smoke from the fires in the cottages, to a dark cluster of buildings at the end of the village. A man named Jim went off to find their horses. He left Henry and Jack standing in the darkness. Dogs barked in the distance.

"You see, Jack, how my family has deserted me."

Henry spoke almost to himself. "My father died. My mother did not stand up to my brother. My sisters married. And now—now even Nanny has had enough."

Jack didn't know what to say.

"It's my own fault," Henry mused. "Too fond of living. I always thought: live for today, not for tomorrow. But tomorrow comes." He paced up and down in the darkness.

"Maybe Lady Marchwell—"

"Aye, maybe. Lady Marchwell or the gallows."

Jack said nothing. There was something self-pitying in Lord Henry. Lady Marchwell or the gallows. Was that how Henry saw his life?

Jim returned with Henry's horse, Red Ruby.

"Is she well?" asked Lord Henry.

"Aye," said Jim.

"When did the soldiers go?"

"A couple hour past."

"Which way?"

"Coast." Jim disliked talk.

"Thank you, Jim."

Lord Henry rubbed Red Ruby's white nose and kissed her and mumbled to her. He led her to a tree stump near the road. Jack followed.

Lord Henry mounted and Jack sat behind him again. He felt bruised from the day before—but he wasn't going to complain, and he clenched his teeth as they trotted up the road to meet the others.

Behind them, they heard a noise: "Ahhh! Go! Go! Bah! Go on! Hup hup."

"What the devil is that horrible noise?" asked Dirty Dick when Jack and Henry arrived.

It was Polly.

She appeared on a little gray pony, coaxing it along the road. It was old and stubborn. She arrived at the meeting place a little after Jack and Henry. She had to coax the pony every step of the way.

"What's the matter?" Polly demanded.

"You're not going to London on that?" laughed Pete the Pudding. He had a sturdy black horse that was snorting with excitement at the thought of being out at night.

"Why not?"

"Looks like that one died about three years ago."

"You'd do better on a cow!" laughed Bernard.

"Never mind," snapped Henry. "We'll discover something on the way. The moon will light us—she is bright tonight and will make the going quick.

Come on." He wheeled Red Ruby around and they set off down the road, hooves drumming on the dirt.

Soon they were traveling fast along a clear white path. Jack hung on for dear life. His bottom crashed painfully into the back of the saddle as he tried to concentrate on each landing. The others followed behind. Every now and then they had to stop and wait for Polly. They could hear her as she approached.

"Go on! You stubborn goat, you old heifer-head! Go! Bah! Go!" When she caught up, they set off again toward the forest.

As they reached the darkness of the trees, they slowed down.

"All right, Jack?" asked Lord Henry.

"Yeah—m-m-mostly," grunted Jack, rigid from the ride.

Lord Henry pulled his horse up short.

"Shhh!"

The others rode up behind. Jack listened and looked around Henry's back, brushing aside the itchy wig. *If only it didn't smell*, he thought. He heard Polly behind, doggedly urging her pony on.

"What is it?" Tom Drum asked.

"Soldiers?" whispered Bernard.

"No. A carriage. Look—a lantern coming this way. Off the road, gang. This is a stroke of luck, indeed."

"Get off the road—we're going to take the carriage," Bernard told Polly as she trotted up.

Chapter Fifteen
Hijack

The light of the carriage came through the dark wood. It looked so little and the darkness all around so big. An owl hooted, and far off its mate returned a lonely cry. Jack's heart was beating with fear and excitement, brought on by danger. He slid off Lord Henry's horse onto the ground, landing in a pile of leaves. He scrambled away, relieved to be off the uncomfortable saddle. He realized how these men were drawn to danger, as a gambler is drawn to cards. The excitement, the thrill—they were irresistible.

Jack found a hiding place among the exposed roots of a tree and burrowed into it. He still had a view of the road but could duck down easily.

Moonlight glimmered through the trees, catching the tops of the tall, silvery trunks but hardly reaching the leafy floor. There was a distinct click of a pistol. Lord Henry urged Red Ruby onto the road.

"Stand and deliver!" he shouted.

"Whoa!" The driver of the carriage slowed his horses. "Who are you?" he called.

> "Henry Vane,
> The very same
> Highwayman of glorious fame."

"Glorious? Notorious is more like it," grumbled the driver of the coach. He opened a little window by his feet and called inside. "We are to be robbed, sire. It is Lord Henry Vane, the polite one, so please—no pistols. He requires only a little money, as a toll."

"Pray—whose coach is this?" Lord Henry inquired.

"Sir Bufton Hart," said the coachman. "The magistrate."

Lord Henry called loudly, "Sir Bufton. Please step out of the carriage."

The door opened and a portly little gentleman stepped down. "I have nothing! No money," he said in a wheedling voice. "Just two shillings. And a few papers. No use to you, I'm afraid. But have what I have. With my blessing." He held out the coins.

"Have what I have?" asked Lord Henry cannily.

"Why, yes, Lord Henry. Have it all. There really is nothing else." He smiled, and this was no doubt the truth, for gentlemen traveling at night sometimes made sure they had little to rob.

"Sir! I wouldn't dream of taking your last two precious shillings," Lord Henry told him, pretending great offense. "Do you take me for a scoundrel?"

"Why no, sir. You are a gentleman."

"The gentleman's master, some say. Have it all, you say?"

"Oh, yes!" Again Sir Bufton held out the two shillings.

"In that case," said Lord Henry with a twinkle in his eye, "I'll take the carriage."

"The carriage? Oh, no, you can't have that! I must get home. I have far to travel. I cannot walk . . ."

"Then you shall ride. Poll!" called Lord Henry. "Hide your face and bring out your steed."

Jack helped Polly cover her face with her scarf, and then she went through the woods with her stubborn gray pony.

"We'll do a swap," said Lord Henry. "You take the pony. We'll take the carriage. You! Coachman! Help your master on this nag. And hand young Poll the reins."

The coachman and the magistrate looked at the tired old pony, then back to the carriage and two horses.

"Impossible!" objected the gentleman. "I have far to go tonight. This beast is old and tired."

"On your way!" Lord Henry barked. His face changed: he was suddenly dangerous, his lip curled, his eyes fierce. "Unless you prefer that we tie you to a tree? We shall leave your carriage and horses at the sign of the Plump Muffin, by Middle Temple. Now be off!"

The magistrate hurriedly climbed onto the pony and set off into the forest with the coachman walking in front. Darkness closed about them, and soon all that could be heard was a far off "Come on! Bah! Go! Go! Hup! Hup!"

Jack rode in the coach while Polly drove. It was comfortable after the horse—but not that comfortable. He bounced around on the hard seat. If only there was a seat belt. He found a leather strap to hold on to and wedged himself in the corner. The carriage had a close, damp, tobacco smell. Bottles in a little side pocket clinked every time they went over a pothole. The wooden seat, with its threadbare covering, and the panels all around the coach creaked and groaned. The wheels ground the gravel on the road. Traveling in a coach was noisier than he'd ever imagined.

After an hour or so, Jack was numb and his arm was tired from holding on. He was relieved when they stopped. He heard voices outside.

"Stand and deliver!" shouted a gruff voice. "Your money or your life!"

At first he thought Lord Henry was robbing another coach. Or perhaps it was a joke. Then he realized: THEY were being robbed! Before he could move, the door opened and a pistol was roughly put against his temple.

"Get down, now!"

"It's a boy!" said a voice.

"Polly," said Jack. "Where's Lord Hen—"

"Quiet!" growled the robber.

"They're ahead," Polly told him in a trembling voice.

"Shut up," cried another robber.

Now Jack wished that he'd never come over to this time. He stumbled out of the coach, the gun at his head. His legs shook. His mouth was dry. He looked up at the moon, bright and high above them, lighting the landscape all around. He saw the faces of the men: they were rough and murderous.

"Empty your pockets!"

Jack fumbled with the strange clothes he was wearing. He couldn't find any pockets. Underneath he still wore his jeans. But in those he had nothing of interest to these robbers. A house key. A twenty-cent piece, a ragged piece of paper from the supermarket.

"Where are you going?" asked one of the men.

Jack didn't have time to answer. Suddenly there was a great thundering of hooves all around them, and the man was knocked flying by a horseman charging between them. Jack dived to the ground. Polly bit the man who was holding her and ran away as another horseman rode between them. There was a sudden BANG! and, in the confusion, someone grabbed Jack and pulled him to the other side of the coach. Dirty Dick held him down.

"Lord Henry Vane!" shouted a familiar voice. "Who are you?"

"John Squires," came the answer, no longer rough and bold—now he was scared. "We didn't know it was you, my lord."

"And your man?"

"Will Goodfellow."

"Low-down, good-for-nothing Tobies!" fumed Lord Henry. "How dare you! You're a disgrace to the profession! No manners! No decency! For goodness sake, man, when you rob a coach: be polite. You don't hold a pistol to the head of a mere boy! Ask first!"

"Yessir!" said one of them.

"Now be on your way!"

"Thank you, sir, thank you." The robbers quickly rode off into the trees. In a few moments they had disappeared into the darkness.

Lord Henry sighed as he tucked away his pistols. "You get all sorts of riffraff near London," he told Jack. "Finchley Common has become quite dreadful."

After this, Jack sat up in the driver's seat with Polly. They both felt safer. Above them, clouds passed slowly over the moon.

"That was nasty," Polly said tight-lipped. "They'd

have shot us for a penny, them two."

"They very nearly did!" Jack reminded her. "At least you know Lord Henry isn't going to kill you."

Polly considered this. "Well, he hasn't killed anyone *yet*. But did you see last night, when he fired his pistol in the air? Twirling it around, like a showman? Imagine if it had hit a passenger? Then we'd have had a problem."

Soon they reached Highgate, a village on a hill to the north of London. From here, they looked down Highgate Hill toward the city of London and the

River Thames, looping like a silver snake in the moonlight.

"Stop! Stop!" cried Jack. He stood up in the driver's seat and gazed at the city in the distance. It was so small. The lights twinkled in the darkness. Here and there small fires burned. "I've been here before," Jack told Polly. "It's near where I live."

In front of them, the road went straight down the hill, past a great lowing and grunting from sheep and pigs and cows that were all in pens ready for the trip to the London market.

Tom Drum rode up with another black cloak and blanket. "Best cover up," he said, tossing them up to Jack. "It's getting cold."

They set off down the hill to the valley below. "This is the Hollow Way," Jack told Polly. "And about here—or there—or near here anyway, is where I live, and the school is over there somewhere." It was difficult to see—there were only dark fields where his school should be—and it made Jack feel giddy imagining the changes that had taken place—or that would take place.

And then they came to London itself. Flaming torches were fixed high up on street corners, and lanterns shone warmly in the windows. In some places, groups of men huddled around braziers of fire, keeping warm in the cool night. So many houses were crowded together and there were open drains in the street. Near the center, people were selling roast meat and pies, calling out their produce. As the highwaymen and the children on the coach picked their way through the twists and turns of the narrow alleys and streets, unfamiliar sounds filled the air.

There were the shouts of men inside the inns and taverns. There was music too, mostly singing or the raw scraping of a fiddle. They saw an argument in the street between two ragged women bawling at each other. Dogs barked. Dogs howled. Dogs slipped silently down side streets. When nine o'clock struck, the city's bells chimed, one and then another and then another. For a full five minutes the air near and far was full of the sound of ringing. And just when they thought it was finished, another one would start.

"It is the best place," said Polly, smiling as if caught in a wonderful dream. "There's nowhere like it. I love it!"

They reached the river, saw the lanterns of the boatmen moving on the dark water, and heard their cries and the splash of oars. Lord Henry muttered that they had gone too far and they turned back.

He finally found the Plump Muffin—an inn near Middle Temple—and disappeared inside while Jack and Polly and the other highwaymen waited in the street. A round woman appeared beside Polly a few minutes later and directed them to the mews, where she could leave the carriage with a man named Thomas. "'E's got barnacles on 'is nose," she said mysteriously.

They found Thomas (whose skin was indeed strangely blistered) and left the carriage with him. Then they went into the Plump Muffin to find Lord Henry. There was a warm and stuffy atmosphere inside the tavern; tobacco smoke and wood fires and cakes and ale all mingled together. The tavern was only half full. A row of little alcoves lay at the end, with benches around each table, enough to seat eight people. Dirty Dick went to a hole in the wall where they served the ale.

"Lord Hen has gone to make inquiries," he told the others, slopping down a jug of ale and some pewter tankards. He poured the foaming brown liquid and took a slurp. "What is he up to?" he asked, mystified.

"I'm in the dark," said Bernard.

"He is following his heart," said Tom Drum. "Lady Marchwell is to be married tomorrow. He is going to tell her that he loves her."

"Oh, he loves her!" said Pete. "I thought something funny were going on."

"And then what?"

"Well, maybe she is going to say, 'Renounce your wicked ways and I will consent to be your bride.'"

"Or—'Go away and never come back!'" laughed Dirty Dick.

"But he's got to try," Jack said, springing to Lord Henry's defense. "Otherwise he'll never know. And he might regret it for the rest of his life."

"Hey," Tom Drum pointed his tankard at Jack, "the boy is wise!"

"Wiser than his years!" agreed Bernard, raising his tankard in a toast.

Dirty Dick laughed. "He'll make a fool of himself, Henry Vane, pandering to a lost lady love. She'll be married tomorrow—and not to some good-for-nothing Toby."

★ ★ ★

Jack felt tired. The exertions of the night and the warm air in the tavern combined to weigh down his eyelids. He found himself watching the candle wax dripping down the pewter holder . . .

"Jack!" Lord Henry was shaking his shoulder. Time had passed and the tavern was almost empty.

"What?"

"Come with me. Now. We shall be back within the hour." Lord Henry winked at the others.

"Good luck, my lord! We shall be here, should you need assistance in your quest," said Tom Drum. He downed the last of his ale and prepared to grab another.

Jack climbed off the bench and followed Lord Henry, who was already striding out of the tavern, his black boots ringing on the broad oak floor.

"What can I do?" Jack asked when they were outside.

"I have a plan," said Lord Henry eagerly. "A grand plan, but elegant too: I want you to appear before Lady Marchwell tonight! As an angel."

Chapter Sixteen
The Divine Messenger

"Me? A what?" Jack was incredulous.

"An angel. I know where she lives. It is on the river and easy to reach. I even know her bedroom. But, were I to appear in her bedroom, I should surely be thrown out, for she will not tolerate my presence. In any case, the bedroom window is too small, and I would get stuck—which would be undignified for a heroic lover such as myself! So my plan is for *you* to appear. Jack, listen, you have fair golden hair, and the pearly skin of a creature from heaven. You look like an angel! You only lack wings. If you were to appear with a letter from me and wings, she would be charmed—she would see it as a vision to astonish."

"You—want—me—to—have—wings?" Jack was amazed and horrified.

"Of course . . . not. Not if you don't want to."

Jack looked at the pleading face of Lord Henry. He was making those big puppy eyes at him again. "But why do you think this will help?"

"Because you have charm, Jack. I believe you can speak to her heart, persuade her to listen. Persuade her thus: that I shall mend my ways. I will do whatever she wants. And I shall honor her. Come on."

"Wait!" Polly came running out of the tavern. "I want to come. Please, can I come? I'll help you. I'll do anything you ask."

Lord Henry looked annoyed. "I didn't ask—," he began.

"I know—but I *want* to help." She gazed up at him and took his hand. She could also turn on the charm, and it wasn't in Henry's heart to turn her away.

"Come on, then," he said, giving in. "I have a boatman waiting."

Polly winked at Jack. He was happy to have her come along, but he was still worried about Lord Henry's plan. He wanted to help Henry, but this felt like a very complicated way to tell someone that you loved them. As they walked toward the Thames, through a series of little alleys with houses teetering over them, Jack could only think that this must be how people declared their love in the eighteenth century.

They reached the river and a boat was waiting. It was small and open and usually used for quick crossing from one bank to the other. The boatman was wrapped in a blanket, but he threw it off when they arrived and set to work. His face was deeply lined, but under his pitiful clothes he was sinewy and strong. He said nothing but rowed hard, and they were soon heading upstream through the silvery moonlit water, past Westminster Abbey and Parliament, out to the large houses beyond. As they went, Lord Henry explained his plan to Jack and Polly.

In half an hour they came within sight of the landing stage of a house with gardens running down to the river. The boatman stowed his oars and they glided silently to the wooden jetty.

"We shall be back in twenty minutes," Lord Henry told the boatman in a low voice. He stepped off the craft. "Wait by the willow tree. If you hear a sharp whistle, then prepare the boat quickly, for we shall want to board and be off directly and at speed."

"Well," said the boatman slowly, "there is an extra charge for departure *at speed*."

"I'll pay double," Henry told him briskly.

The boatman agreed and slipped away, leaving the three of them on the jetty. Lord Henry was carrying a sack that he must have stowed in the boat when he first hired it.

"What have you got there?" asked Jack suspiciously.

"Come. I'll show you." Lord Henry walked through an arch at the end of the jetty, into a beautiful walled garden. Jack and Polly followed. The house beyond was framed by two tall trees. It was old and large with a dozen or so little windows. A vine, now bare of leaves, twisted over one end of it.

"Here." Lord Henry opened the sack and carefully brought out a pair of beautiful white swan's wings. They almost shone in the moonlight. "Aren't they something? I got them from a lady friend at the Drury Lane Theatre."

"I can't—," began Jack.

"You really will look like an angel!" Polly laughed and clapped her hands.

"You will," said Lord Henry beaming with pleasure at Polly's reaction. "Why—even better, you could be Cupid. The messenger of the god of love. She will adore that! Here, put this white smock on first. Now, this strap belongs here and this attaches here . . ."

"I feel stupid," said Jack. He tried to think of a reason for not doing this, but he couldn't. He said he'd help Henry, and he had always thought that loyalty was important.

"You look heavenly," said Henry. "You are indeed my divine messenger. Angel Jack."

Polly was enjoying the fun, grinning at Jack and admiring him. At least, she was until Lord Henry turned and said, "Now you, Polly." Her smile disappeared. "You said you would do anything."

"I did," she said guardedly, her eyes narrowing.

"Go around the front and keep watch."

"Is that it?" She was disappointed.

"Yes," Lord Henry told her. "If you hear anything, anything at all, then come right back. I shall whistle when all is done."

Polly slipped away, leaving Henry with the Angel Jack. It didn't sound right to Jack. There was no Angel Jack in the Bible, at least as far as he knew.

And real angels appeared in a blaze of light. They didn't creep up on people when they were asleep. Swan's wings, a smock, and fair hair? What hope did he have?

Lord Henry handed Jack a lantern with a little sliding door that opened to show the light. As he opened the lantern door, his large face was lit up. Jack saw his smile, his strong chin, and his big, warm eyes.

"You will do it, won't you?" Henry asked. "You are my last hope."

"Oh, all right." Jack was unable to resist this plea. He was in Lord Henry's hands—if Henry wanted Jack to do something ridiculous, then so be it. "Don't blame me if it doesn't work," he warned.

Lord Henry gave Jack one more run through of all that he was supposed to say and handed him a note to give to Lady Marchwell. Creeping through the fallen leaves, they approached the house. Lord Henry pointed out the window Jack had to climb to. It didn't look that high up, just ten easy steps up a strong vine. The window was already open a crack.

"Good luck. Persuade her well."

Jack set off, like his namesake up the beanstalk,

from gnarled trunk to twisted branch, up and up, higher and higher.

The window was narrow and squeaked as he opened it. But he managed to put the little lantern onto a windowsill and squeeze through into the room. He went head first and landed softly behind a thick curtain (*not the usual angelic arrival*, he thought ruefully). Standing up with a rustling of wings, he waved to Lord Henry below, who waved back cheerily and clutched his heart dramatically.

You owe me a favor, Jack thought grimly, as he took a deep breath and prepared to enter the room.

Drawing aside the curtain, he stepped into the darkness. *Everything is dark in this time,* he thought. Not just dark but pitch-black. They could do with a streetlight here and there. He opened the door of the lantern just a crack. The thin beam of light lit up a big red velvet shape in the middle of the room and a chair and a dressing table. A door. A chest. The big velvet shape was the bed. It was a four-poster and the curtains were drawn. *Even darker in there*, he guessed.

He tiptoed over to the end of the bed and opened one of the curtains a crack.

"My lord?" mumbled a figure inside the bed. "Is

that you? Is something wrong?" It was a woman's voice. For an awful moment Jack wondered if he had the right person.

Don't think, just do it. Do it, Jack told himself firmly.

He pulled the curtain fully open and then slid the door of the lantern. Light spilled onto the bed, lighting up Lady Marchwell and the bedclothes. She let out a small cry, and Jack began the speech he had prepared:

"My lady, please excuse this visit, but I come from afar and with . . . um . . . a message: I know one

who loves you. He has always loved you. He loved you from afar. And wants you to be his."

"Wait—you frighten me!" she scolded and, clasping her hand to her chest, she retreated up the bed, clutching the covers around her. She frowned at him, disbelievingly. Jack saw a young, pretty woman in a lace bonnet with blue eyes and rosy cheeks— the woman whom he had seen robbed only yesterday. Her frown gave way to a small smile. Jack was relieved she wasn't scared. He certainly would have been if a boy in swan's wings had appeared at the bottom of *his* bed.

"Are you an angel?" she asked, mystified and amused. Jack felt her eyes traveling over him. "Is it a play?" she asked.

"Well, no. Or sort of," he said. He supposed it was a bit like a school nativity play. He noticed the lantern shaking in his hand.

"I come from afar," he said again. Oh, he hated drama! He was just no good at pretending like this. He hated that feeling of making a fool of himself, of feeling so exposed.

Lady Marchwell shook her head and smiled. She *was* amused! "Why, what silliness is this, to send a Cupid on my wedding eve? That my lord should suddenly be so thoughtful after being so cold and harsh! It does make me warm to him! And I had thought to call the wedding off! Sweet boy—I am in need of sleep—for surely my lord does not want to marry some tired wretch tomorrow morn?"

"Me? Oh, I see. My, er, lord," began Jack, realizing something was not quite right, "has written you a note."

He handed it over.

Lady Marchwell took the note. Jack held up the lantern so that she could read it. He wished she would hurry up, then he could go, his job done. But he watched in alarm as the color drained from her rosy cheeks. Her face lost its merry delight. "Oh!" She groaned and closed her eyes. She slapped the note down on the bed. "It is Lord Henry."

"Yes. That's right," said Jack. It dawned on him that Lady Marchwell had thought he was an angel sent by the Honorable Hogg, the man she was to marry. From the way she had said "Lord Henry," he could not tell if she was struck with horror or with relief. She was struck with something. Surprise— that was for sure.

The silence lengthened and Jack felt more and more awkward. Everything hung in the balance.

Jack continued to wish he was somewhere else. Anywhere else. Anywhere at all. He heard a creaking noise nearby. Was that someone at the door? He prepared to run for it. *Hurry up*, he thought.

At last Lady Marchwell spoke in a small, sad voice: "Lord Henry Vane." Jack waited. "I heard he was at Wittlesham, with his nanny."

"That's right," said Jack.

Nothing else came from her, except a sigh.

Jack felt awkward. Now was the time to persuade her. He spoke quickly. "He says he has always loved you, only he never managed to tell you. And he wishes that he had. Told you, that is. Because if he had, then everything might be different. And that's why he sent me, to . . . to . . . tell you."

There was more silence. At last, with a noise that was really a howl, she cried in anguish, "How *could* he?"

And before she could say more, there was a sudden, terrible cry from the direction of the window—followed by a loud crack and a tearing noise. Jack spun around. Abandoning Lady Marchwell, he ran to the window and looked out.

Below in the garden, Lord Henry was lying on his back on the lawn. The large old vine lay broken around him. He held the thick trunk of the vine in his hand. Jack looked down at where the vine had been. There was nothing. It had gone.

"Help," he whispered hoarsely, for now he felt he had done all he could and must be away. Quickly. Only, how would he get down?

"I was listening," explained Henry uselessly, "but the vine—it wouldn't hold me. It came away from the wall. Stupid thing!" He rubbed his back as he began clambering out from the debris, kicking aside the tangled branches.

"What do *I* do?" whispered Jack desperately. He could hear Lady Marchwell stirring behind him. Far off in the house a door banged.

Henry struggled to his feet and looked around for something with which he could help Jack—a ladder perhaps or a long pole. He brushed down his cloak and adjusted his hair. "Sorry, Jack," he apologized. "I think you'd better, er . . . hide?" he suggested. "I'll be back. I promise!"

At that moment Jack saw two figures running around the side of the building. "Watch out!" he cried.

Henry spun around, saw the men, and took off in the direction of the river. Jack watched him go, his cloak flapping, his hand on his head holding onto his hat and wig as he whistled loudly for the boatman.

Jack hid behind the curtain, shaking. That was it. He was alone now. Great. Fantastic. What exactly was he supposed to do? Where could he hide? There was nowhere. He was stuck. This was a catastrophe. A curtain! It was the most obvious place in the world to hide.

A second later someone burst into Lady Marchwell's room. Jack saw light flickering around the edge of the curtains. A man demanded of Lady Marchwell if she was all right. As Jack listened, he saw his shoes were sticking out. Slowly he tried to withdraw them.

A second later, he was roughly grabbed.

He dropped the lantern with a cry and his wings were crushed.

Chapter Seventeen

Capture!

Jack struggled in vain. A big bear of a man hugged him until he could hardly breathe. He was locked in the man's arms, his face squashed and scratched by the rough material of the sleeves. He was unable to speak. An older man came over with a lantern and held it in Jack's face.

"Who's this rascal?" he asked.

Jack looked beyond the lantern to the man's face and saw he had a drooping eyelid, a slurred mouth, and a red nightcap on his head. The man scowled at Jack and then reached out and grabbed his cheek. He squeezed until it hurt.

"Leave him," said Lady Marchwell quickly.

"He did no harm to me."

"I shall deliver him to the constable, madam. Directly."

"Wait until the morning," ordered Lady Marchwell. "When his lordship arrives. We can deal with him then."

A maid rushed in with another lantern and began making a fuss over Lady Marchwell, demanding to know what had happened—and this on the eve of her wedding—was she all right? Did he, God forbid, come near her or make demands? Was the trousseau untouched and the jewelry safe?

Jack was carried out by the bear, who marched him down a dark hallway. Jack's legs dangled, knocking against the man's shins. The hallway was paneled in dark wood, with rows of portraits that swam in and out of vision as the pool of lantern light passed by. They went down a staircase. There were dogs barking somewhere, and the older man went ahead calling to the dogs, calming them. Before Jack could see much more of his surroundings, he was thrown roughly into an empty closet. The door banged shut, leaving him in darkness. More darkness. The key turned.

Jack lay still, trying to calm down, trying to think

straight. He took deep, steady breaths. He angrily pulled off the swan's feathers, flung them down, and buried his face in his hands. He would not let himself cry.

He had been there for a couple of minutes, his head in his hands, wondering what was to become of him, when he heard a hubbub. As the voices came closer he recognized Polly's, and he could tell from her cries and grunts that she was struggling. Despite himself he was relieved to discover he was not going to be alone. At least she was captured too. He heard her resisting for all she was worth. A moment later the door was unlocked, and the little bundle of Polly was thrown in roughly.

"I done nothing," she cried. "You stinking heap of aaach!" She spat and spat again on the floor.

The door banged shut.

"Polly!" whispered Jack. He reached out and found her arm. "You all right?"

"Yeah. You too, Jack?" she said. "That big troll— you know the one?—he bumped smack into me and grabbed me as I was running from the other one."

"What did you do?" asked Jack.

"I bit him."

"Good." Jack smiled. He could imagine Polly's fury and her sharp teeth.

She gave a hollow little laugh. "Well, they got me and they got you, and lucky Lord Henry escapes again! How does he do it? He's like a slippery eel." She slumped against the wall and groaned. "What happened to you?"

Jack told her. Polly chuckled when she heard how Lord Henry had pulled down the vine and landed in the garden. "What a bumpkin! He'll never hear the end of this!"

"What if we're sent to prison for burglary?" Jack asked.

"No—Henry will spring us."

"What do you mean?

"Rescue us. He is a man of honor."

"Honor? How can he be a man of honor? He's a highwayman." Jack felt annoyed at Henry. In his mind's eye, he saw him retreating to the river with his hand holding onto his hat and wig.

"Yeah, but he will look after us. I have faith."

"Do you? You should have seen how quickly he left."

"Oh? Well, mostly I have faith," she said after thinking. "Anyway, he is our only hope. So it's a

151

good thing for us he is as slippery as an eel."

Jack agreed. He found that he could just see the outline of Polly in the almost complete darkness. "Where do you think we are?" he whispered.

"I don't know—I think it is a pantry or something." Polly began feeling the walls, tapping them with her hand. "There's a little window up there, and there's herbs drying."

"And this wall here is warm," said Jack. "It must be near the fire."

"Behind it, I think." Polly was feeling all around the door frame. "Fizzle heads! We are well and truly stuck," she declared.

They sat there for an hour. Maybe two. Jack wished many times that he had worn his watch. If he ever got out he promised himself that he would always wear it—in bed, in the shower, in the swimming pool. He would never take it off. It might look strange with the rough, itchy clothes he was wearing, but he longed to know the time. He wondered what Granny was doing now—and then put it out of his mind. He didn't want to think of that.

Together they waited for the sound of the rescue party. They talked about their favorite things (Jack liked chocolate muffins, soccer, and sledding; Polly liked toast and jam, country fairs, and long summer evenings), and they talked about the things they wanted to do: Jack wanted to sail around the world; Polly wanted to have sixty head of cattle and a house of her own. They talked about the best things in the eighteenth century and the best things in the twenty-first, and they decided that they each liked their own best. Time passed and their hopes dwindled.

At last they heard footsteps and low voices outside in the hallway. The key turned in the lock and, surprisingly quickly, the big man reached in and grabbed each of them by the arm.

"Ow, that hurts," cried Jack.

"So keep still," growled the man, pulling them both out like rag dolls.

He hauled them along a dark hallway, through the paneled entrance hall, and past the staircase then stopped before a large oak door. Holding the children in front of him, he knocked.

"Come in."

He pushed open the door and it creaked on its hinges. Jack and Polly felt the man prod them in the back and they walked forward into another fine room, where there was a long table with chairs running down each side. There was an oil lamp on the table and beyond it a figure in a cloak stood looking out of the window. The faintest glimmer of dawn was visible in the east.

She turned around. It was Lady Marchwell.

"Leave us," she told the servant, and she watched him go before turning to look at the children.

She was wearing a long black dress and over it a cloak. She looked ready to go out. Her hair was drawn tightly into a bun and little ringlets framed her face. As she looked at Jack and Polly, she let out a long sigh.

"Children, who are you?"

They told her their names.

"And how old are you?"

"I'm nine, beggin' your pardon, marm," said Polly.

"I'm ten," said Jack. "Marm," he mumbled as an afterthought, though it didn't sound quite right.

Lady Marchwell shook her head. She obviously thought this was a very sad affair. "What foolishness!" she tutted. "That this should happen on the very eve of my wedding. You are friends of Henry?"

"Yes," they replied.

Jack watched her face. She looked stern and strong, he thought, different from the woman confronted by a boy-angel in her bed.

"Henry Vane claims to be honorable, brave, and fair—yet he uses children to woo for him. Children to break into houses for him. Children to rob for him. How utterly . . . low."

"We weren't robbing—honestly," said Jack.

"I don't think the magistrate will think that. I think the magistrate will find you guilty and will have you quickly dispatched. A whipping—or worse: you know you could be hanged for this? On the other hand," she mused, "you don't look like robbers."

"I never been a robber, ever," said Polly. "I was just helping Lord Henry."

"He paid you well, I trust?"

"No. He is a friend. We didn't do it for a payment, we did it for a favor. Didn't we, Jack?"

Jack nodded. "I thought it was fun," he said, though somehow "fun" didn't sound like the right word, considering the trouble they were in, and Jack wished he hadn't said it.

Lady Marchwell's face softened. "Indeed, in a manner, it was fun," she said and Jack felt better, as she didn't seem to be blaming him. "But perhaps it also had a serious purpose?" She searched Jack's eyes as if seeking confirmation of her thoughts. Or did she think there was something strange about him?

"I think he meant every word," Jack stammered. "I'm sure he did."

"He is not a bad man," said Polly.

"You care about him, do you?" asked Lady Marchwell.

"I do," said Polly stoutly.

Jack nodded agreement.

"Let me tell you about Henry," she said with a sigh. "I knew him as a child. He always had a strange aura about him. He has it now—a presence that makes people like him. However much people disapprove of what he is and what he does, they still like him. He charms them, with his smile and his foolishness and his gallantry. Oh, for a single smile they will forgive any betrayal or any thoughtlessness or meanness."

Polly nodded; she recognized this description.

"But they do him no favors," Lady Marchwell continued, "for see how he abuses their love now—running amok on the highways of England. Robbing people and pretending it is all a game of daring. Only now the tide is turning. People are growing tired of the stories of his robberies, and soon they will hate him and wish him all manner of ills. He will be caught and hanged for sure, unless he changes his ways."

Lady Marchwell approached the two children, and then, surprising even herself, she let them in on a secret: "And yet I too am under his spell. I had put him out of my mind as firmly as I could, but since he robbed me the other night, I have thought of him often. And now that he is back in my life, I must help him. It is time he was taught a lesson. For his own good."

Jack understood Lady Marchwell. He found that he liked her and he believed her. Her blue eyes were shining as she looked at the two children—hopeful and pleading at the same time. He glanced at Polly. She was staring at Lady Marchwell. Were they being asked to betray Lord Henry?

"It is your choice," Lady Marchwell urged. "I can have you taken straight to the magistrate and committed to Newgate Prison—or you can join me now in playing such a trick on Lord Henry Vane that he will never dare commit highway robbery again."

Newgate Prison? Jack didn't think it sounded appealing at all.

"What have you in mind, marm?" Polly spoke like an innocent child, but Jack knew her better.

"That we give Lord Henry Vane a dose of his own medicine. There are only two ways to this house: by the river or by the Lambeth Road. If I am not mistaken, he will come to find you by the road. And if you agree, we shall be waiting for him. And we shall show him *exactly* what it is like to be robbed. What do you say?"

Jack and Polly turned to each other. Polly was smiling. Jack saw she was won over. It was a better deal than going to the magistrate, certainly—but was it betrayal?

Polly spoke: "If it saves him, then . . ."

"It's not betrayal. It would be for his own good," said Jack slowly, and Polly nodded.

Lady Marchwell inclined her head. "What do you say, then?"

"Yes—I mean, yes, marm," he said.

"Good." She smiled and put out her hand. "It is a deal."

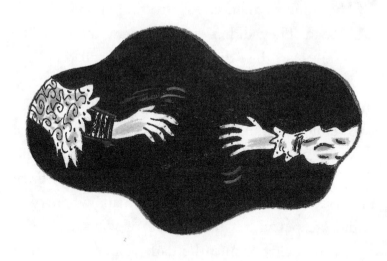

Chapter Eighteen
A Lesson in Robbery

The highwaymen were trotting along Surrey Road. They didn't want to draw attention to themselves, so they didn't gallop. But still they had to be quick. Lord Henry had explained that they might need to break into the house to rescue the two children. They might have to hold up the servants and get them to show them to Jack and Polly. The others didn't like the sound of that. They preferred robbery on the open road, where you could escape with a quick kick of your heels, out across the fields or into the dark woods. In a house there were all sorts of problems. Furniture to trip over. People hiding behind doors. Dogs.

However, this was special. It was Jack and Polly, members of the Vane Gang, so they had to do something, didn't they?

The road followed the course of the river and the houses along it. Sometimes there were fences and fields, sometimes the long wall of a great house marking out its boundary. All the time the sky was slowly lightening. At one place the road narrowed by an old barn and sharply turned left between the walls of two of the big estates. Lady Marchwell's house was just beyond, and the highwaymen slowed down.

No sooner were they walking between the walls than there was a cry.

"Stand and deliver! Put your hands above your heads or I fire!"

A horseman appeared suddenly in the road, two long-barreled pistols primed and pointing straight at them.

"I don't believe it," grumbled Lord Henry. He obediently put his hands above his head; the others followed. "Who are you?" he called out angrily.

"A robber," replied the robber coldly. Blue eyes blinked behind a mask.

"Well, well," said Tom Drum. "I'd never have guessed."

"Quiet!" The robber pointed a pistol directly at Tom Drum.

"Do you know who I am?" asked Lord Henry.

"No."

"I am Lord Henry Vane. Highwayman of glorious fame."

"Wow!" came a youthful voice from behind them. "I'm impressed."

Henry glanced around. There were two more masked robbers. Rude and cheeky robbers. This was tricky. They were blocking their escape route. How absolutely tiresome.

The first robber laughed gently. "Lord Henry Vane, the man who should be quite ashamed!"

One of the cheeky robbers joined in: "Lord Henry Vane, who caused us all a deal of pain! Ha, ha!"

"Just a minute!" objected Lord Henry. "This isn't a poetry contest! I've got important things to do."

"And so do we, Lord Vane," said the first robber, suddenly quite fierce. "Everyone—throw down your pistols, dismount, and take off your pants, boots, and coats!"

"What?" gasped Henry.

"My new boots?" cried Tom Drum.

"You want my 'orrible smelly pants?" groaned Bernard.

"Yes! No! *I* don't want them. They are to be given to the poor," the robber replied smartly. "*I* want your jewels and your horses."

There was silence. The highwaymen didn't move. Pants? Horses? There were limits. Their hands were still held above their heads. The first robber now moved forward and, taking Henry by surprise, suddenly pointed the long-barreled pistol directly at his heart. Henry felt the barrel of the gun against his rib. There was a click. A small squeeze of the trigger and Henry would be dead.

Henry Vane knew those pistols. They were unstable. Often they fired accidentally.

Henry Vane was not a coward, but he looked into the eyes of the masked robber in front of him and he felt fear. On his forehead beads of cold sweat gathered, and in the cold dawn light his face was gray. Still he held his hands aloft. They shook gently. The barrel nudged against his heart.

"This is how they feel, Henry," said the robber softly.

"Who?"

"The people you rob."

"I never hurt them," said Henry weakly.

"Yes, you do. You hurt them by frightening them." The robber's blue eyes burned into Henry's. Henry blinked to break the accusing stare and looked down at the gun.

"Yes," he agreed. "I do frighten them."

The highwaymen were silent. The robbers were silent too.

Very slowly, the first robber removed her mask. Her stern expression seemed gentler and softer without the mask. Henry Vane opened his mouth and closed it. No sound came out. She withdrew the pistol. Henry's hands, quivering above his head, drifted down. He nodded, understanding at last. The other two robbers—the children—also removed

their masks, and then all the highwaymen's hands dropped down and they sat in the gathering light, their horses shifting uneasily under them.

"Very funny," said Dirty Dick.

"Oh, I see!" said Tom Drum. "It's—ha, ha!—Jack and Polly," he laughed, "and Lady—er—hum."

"Well," said Henry. "Well. Well. Well."

"Well, what?" asked Lady Marchwell.

Lord Henry pursed his lips. His mouth twitched but he couldn't quite smile. He was a fool. An utter, utter fool.

"What a trick! What a *funny* trick to play. Ha. Really fooled me. Yes—how very . . . *frivolous.* Funny joke, Jack! Funny joke, Polly!" He winked at the two children.

Jack smiled sheepishly. He watched Lord Henry struggle with his feelings. He was angry and hurt. He had been coming to rescue them, Jack thought. Which was honorable. But then this had happened. Now he was shaken.

"It's not a joke, Henry. It's a lesson. Will you change?" asked Lady Marchwell.

Henry looked past her. The sun would rise soon. Another day would begin.

"Yes," he said at last. "I will. My days as a high-wayman are over."

"If you do . . . ," she began.

"You will marry me?" Lord Henry ventured, attempting his old confidence.

Lady Marchwell sighed. "No," she said. "But I will help you gain a pardon."

They accompanied Lady Marchwell back to the house. The highwaymen were soon in good spirits. Jack sensed that they were relieved. Everything was put back to where it had been; all was right again. Only Lord Henry was changed. His spirit had shrunk. The men talked about their feelings of surprise that there had been robbers on the road at that time in the morning; how peculiar they had thought it that the robbers had high voices and that the two little ones wore cloaks almost to the ground. Rascals! But the sight of the long-barreled pistol pointing straight at the heart of Lord Henry had truly alarmed them.

"When I sees you with the gun," said Dirty Dick, his eyes all wide and dramatic, "then I was thinking that this were going to end in some bloody way and I got ready to spur my horse and jump the wall."

"Those pistols fire with the littlest touch of the trigger, they do," said Pete the Pudding.

"It wasn't loaded," Lady Marchwell told them. "I would never have shot Henry. He is a little too precious." She glanced at him fondly.

Lord Henry managed a wan smile. Jack could see he was feeling low. But if he could escape the hangman's noose, surely that would make him happy? Henry Vane, usually so much larger than life, sat on Red Ruby with his head bowed and his shoulders slumped forward. Jack worried. Was Lord Henry Vane going to deflate like an old balloon or square up to the battle of life?

Chapter Nineteen
The Flight for Life

Jack had to go home. The sun would soon be up, and they were still two hours' ride from Wittlesham. As they reached the gates to Lady Marchwell's house, all the horses stopped abruptly. Stuck at the back, Jack stood in his stirrups to see why they had stopped.

In the driveway stood a magnificent green and gold carriage bedecked in white flowers, with six matching gray horses. It was the carriage that was to take Lady Marchwell to the church.

"Look at that!" gasped Polly.

"My! That is grand," said Bernard, rolling his eyes.

But Lady Marchwell was vexed. "They are early.

Far too early. You had better stay out of sight. I have more than enough explanations to give for the events of tonight."

"Why, that is a beauty!" said Lord Henry softly. He was at his most generous—no trace of envy in his voice. "You will be the most radiant bride in all England."

Lady Marchwell smiled at Lord Henry's kindness, but her eyes returned to the carriage with a troubled look.

She bit her lip. "It is too much," she muttered. "I did not ask for this. I am forever pushed into things I do not want." She changed the subject. "Will you be returning to Wittlesham?"

They said they would, and right away. Lord Henry said that they must be careful because the soldiers were still searching for them. It would not be easy. Once they reached Wittlesham they would be safe, for they had a wonderful hideout there.

"Jack and I could go on our own," Polly suggested. "It is dangerous for you all to come. Specially as it's daylight."

"No," cried Tom Drum, "I would like to come!"

"Me too," said Dirty Dick. "We must come."

"We have to—to protect you from robbers . . ."

"And other bad people . . ."

"The trouble is," Jack said, "that you all look like highwaymen with your black cloaks and hats. You stick out a mile. It'd be much easier if you looked like something else. Like farmers or merchants or beggars . . . or . . ." But he couldn't think of anything else.

"Or a wedding party," said Lady Marchwell, gazing at the coach.

In the silence that followed, Henry Vane sat up straighter and straighter in the saddle. He seemed to grow in front of them. He jutted his chin out in a determined fashion and pursed his lips. He looked neither right nor left but stared straight at the wedding carriage and six gray horses. There was hope. A glimmer of hope. *Life is returning*, thought Jack with pleasure.

"But, Lady Marchwell—," he said a little formally, "how *will* you get to church?"

"At this moment," she hesitated and took a decisive breath, "I think a ride in the countryside would be preferable to church. It is a terrible thing to do, I know, to miss church . . . and yet . . ." She looked at Henry, and he understood.

"Fresh air is what you need!" said Tom Drum lustily.

"Yes," she agreed. "But I do feel bad. I feel disloyal and rebellious."

"There's nothing so delicious as a little rebellion," said Lord Henry, and he smiled a truly beautiful smile.

Lady Marchwell blushed. "Oh, no, what am I thinking? Truly I can't," she said, wavering.

"But you can," urged Henry passionately. "You would be doing nothing wrong, Emily, for missing church can be the right thing sometimes. Forgive me for saying so, but Hogg, this man—this *Hogg*—he is not right for you, Emily. He is old and dull and pompous and not even very good looking. I mean, do take time to consider, if you are unsure."

Now Jack worried that Henry had gone too far. Lady Marchwell would not be pushed. She had to make up her own mind.

"Let's do it!" she cried suddenly. She spurred her horse forward and set off at a canter toward the carriage. Lord Henry did the same.

"What's she doing?" cried Dirty Dick.

"She's stealing the carriage," said Jack excitedly.

"What? Why?" asked Bernard.

"Because she's not getting married today," Jack explained. "She has had second thoughts. She is coming with us to Wittlesham."

"She is going to take us in that carriage!" squealed Polly. "Disguised as a wedding party!"

They watched as Lord Henry charged up to the carriage, wheeled around it, then, like a circus acrobat, sprung from Red Ruby straight into the driver's seat. He unhooked the reins and helped Lady Marchwell on board. The footmen and coach drivers were inside the house, unaware of the theft of their vehicle.

Henry released the brake and shook the reins, and the six horses and the carriage trundled forward. The flowers quivered at first and then, as they gathered speed, shook vigorously. It was a magnificent sight, the six horses stamping and snorting and shaking their manes, the shiny carriage moving down the avenue of trees. Here was the eighteenth-century equivalent, thought Jack, of a stretch limo. As they came closer, he saw Lady Marchwell laughing and Henry grinning like a boy.

They brought the carriage thundering past the highwaymen and out onto the road. No one at the house appeared to have noticed. Henry stood up in the driver's seat and drove the horses forward, suddenly quite carried away, cracking the whip in the air and whooping with joy. His spirits were soaring! After a mile, he stopped and the others caught up.

Finding footmen's uniforms in the back of the carriage, the highwaymen transformed themselves into servants. They had green and gold jackets and strange little hats and pantaloons. Dressed up, they looked a bit like frogs. Jack, Polly, Henry, and Lady Marchwell sat inside the plush carriage. Tom Drum drove with Pete the Pudding next to him. Bernard stood at the back, bursting out of his green pants and short jacket and graciously bowing to everyone they passed. Dirty Dick rode behind, holding the reins of their horses until they could find a place to leave them.

"Oh, my, this is comfortable!" gushed Polly, stroking the velvet seats.

"We are like jewels in a box," said Lord Henry sweetly.

Jack thought it was the most uncomfortable carriage in the world. Riding his bike down a staircase would be more comfortable. And his bed at Granny's was quieter.

"Keep a steady pace, Tom," cried Lord Henry as they came to the city and crossed London Bridge. People were beginning to stir; they were setting up their stalls, calling out their wares, bells ringing, carts full of produce arriving for the day's work. As they came up to Highgate, there were sheep and cattle jostling in the middle of the road—but everyone made way for them, gawking at the magnificent carriage, wondering who the special people inside were.

Pete the Pudding bowed to them. Bernard waved and grinned from the back. Tom Drum told him to behave properly.

"Coachmen are very snooty," he shouted to Bernard. "Put yer nose in the air and pretend they smell."

"They do smell," said Bernard.

"An' do up yer trousers—they're rude," shouted Dirty Dick at the back.

"If I do them up, they'll split like a pea pod," Bernard retorted.

They crossed Finchley Common and continued up Great North Road. Inside the carriage, shaken, rattled, and bumped, Jack drifted in and out of sleep. He felt so tired. *Sleep is the best way to get through journeys*, he thought. *Close your eyes and . . . arrive. Journey over.*

He woke up suddenly. They were approaching a group of soldiers. Tom Drum's face suddenly appeared in a little door above his seat: "There's soldiers ahead!" he said fearfully.

"Keep going," said Lady Marchwell firmly. "Don't stop unless they tell you to. Salute them and continue, with absolute confidence!"

"Yes, marm," said Tom Drum.

Everyone made themselves as presentable as possible.

The grand carriage approached. The soldiers hesitated. They peered at the carriage, at the liveried coachmen, at the very important persons staring straight ahead . . . and decided that they did not want to stop them. Must be some fancy wedding.

"Yes!" cried Lord Henry when they were clear. "It works!"

They continued on toward Wittlesham, and Jack listened as Henry and Lady Marchwell discussed how they would secure a pardon for Lord Henry and his gang. But Jack couldn't hear very well over the rattle of the carriage and fell asleep, before waking again to hear Lady Marchwell speaking sternly about the future.

"You have to pay back the people you robbed, with the money you *earn*," she was telling Henry forcefully. "All your life, Henry, you have either been given money, or you have taken money. That has to change. You have to *earn* it."

She was really being quite hard on him. Her face was set. Lord Henry squirmed.

"But how?" he bleated.

"Hard work!" Lady Marchwell stressed the words. "You earn money by offering a service: being a lawyer or a doctor or a soldier or a farmer or buying and selling goods or making something that other people want. There are so many things you can do, if you put your mind to it."

"Absolutely," said Henry. "One good idea and you're off." His eyes fell on Jack across from him in the carriage. Jack wondered what idea Henry might have. A showman perhaps. Or a businessman. But then Henry winked, and Jack guessed that he already had an idea. Probably one that didn't involve too much work.

As he watched them, Jack was reminded of his mom and dad. Mom was the one with the ideas, but Dad went ahead and did what he wanted anyway. Where were they now, he wondered. He held onto the strap and looked out of the side window at the countryside rushing by—the fields and trees and walls and fences and the woods drenched in the early morning light, the grass sparkling with dew . . . and then he drifted off to sleep again.

"Jack!" Lord Henry shook him awake. Polly and Lady Marchwell had their eyes closed. They were asleep now. Only Henry was excited. He leaned forward and took Jack's hands in his. He spoke over the noise of the carriage. "I must thank you," he said, "for winning over Lady Marchwell. For your angelic work. You are my mascot, Jack, my lucky charm."

"That's okay," said Jack sleepily. "It's been fun. I like it here, but I really have to get back."

"Of course, Jack, of course. But listen to me: I have an idea. A very fine and interesting idea. I should like to propose a business partnership between you and me."

"A *business* partnership?"

"Indeed." He glanced at the others to make sure they weren't listening. "You remember that Dick sold a shilling for seventy-five pounds? Well, he told me there was all manner of old things in the 'antiques' shop. There were pistols and glasses and plates and chairs and . . . and even bed-warming pans! Ha! Things that I could get here and—what do you think?—I could bring them over to your time and sell them. Think of the money! And there are things in your time that would be very useful here: like . . . blow-dryers. And that nice flashlight that the constable had. And the yummy chocolate bars. We could be 'time traders'! Vane and Bolt! What do you think, eh?"

Jack stared at Lord Henry. How changed he was. And suddenly Jack thought—what a *brilliant* idea!

"We could do time *tours*!" cried Henry. "Tours of London in the twenty-first century! Even the king would come! Come and see Granny Bolt's house!

And the future. Come and see the future! What fun! A guinea a visit."

"I could bring my class," Jack told him. "And all the newspapers and TV. And we could bring you electricity so your lives would be better. And food— we could bring you better food. And medicine—our medicine is much better than yours. And cars and trains and planes—they are all so much better. And better roads. And what would your king say about a computer? It would knock his socks off!"

"Eh?" Henry looked puzzled. "Of course it would all be better, wouldn't it? I suppose you have better pistols too?"

"Pistols?" Jack laughed. "We've got an atomic bomb! We can destroy the world with that! It's *huge*."

"Goodness," said Henry, his brows knitted together.

"And you could go to the moon."

"*The moon?*"

"Yup. Humans have been to the moon. Soon any-one will be able to go to the moon."

"But what for?" asked Henry.

"For the experience," said Jack. "To experience life. That's what we're here for."

"Are we? Henry stroked the carriage seat as he digested the implications of his business proposal. He imagined bringing a car through the little hole in Jack's bedroom. Or a road. It all looked extremely complicated. "I quite like carriages, you know. And horses. I like beautiful, strong horses like Red Ruby. I like them much more than cars. Maybe we should take it . . . you know . . . step-by-step?"

"Okay," said Jack.

Five minutes later he leaned forward again. "You know, Jack, I think it most interesting that the only building in Wittlesham to have survived two hundred and fifty years is the Cap and Stockings!"

Jack smiled. There were other buildings too, but Henry was right. People always needed a pub.

"To be an innkeeper," continued Henry, "must be a fine way to earn money. For it is work that will never go out of fashion!"

"Indeed," agreed Jack, still thinking of all the advances he could bring to Henry's world.

"You know, I noticed that the beams in the Cap and Stockings are exactly the same in your time as in our time. They lasted unchanged for two hundred and fifty years! I wonder what would happen if we carved our names on the beams in the Cap and Stockings? Maybe they would suddenly appear over in your time. We should try that! It would be most interesting. Indeed, things we change here could have very strange consequences over two hundred and fifty years. All your cars and computers. The whole of history could change," he mused, and he fell into a thoughtful silence.

As they passed over the common, Jack suddenly recognized the road into Wittlesham. He marveled again at how changed it was. How sleepy and quiet, how rural. A man was driving two horses and a plow across a field. A boy began running alongside the carriage, barefoot, in dirty clothes, waving excitedly to them. Jack saw apples on the trees and haystacks in the fields and huge flocks of birds gathering to migrate.

As they entered the village, there was a lot of activity—cows in the road and people running here and there carrying tubs and buckets. The carriage slowed to a crawl.

"There's a fire in the village," Tom Drum called down to them.

Polly leaped out of her seat. "Where?" she cried.

"Make way. Make way!" cried Tom Drum.

"Where is it?" cried Polly.

"'Tis the house—'tis Nanny Manners's house!"

cried Tom Drum. "Make way! Make way!"

Jack felt his head swim. He suddenly knew he had to get back. He had to get back quickly. He looked at Polly and at Lord Henry. Lord Henry realized too.

"Jack—we have to get you back," Henry said urgently.

"We've got to help!" cried Polly.

The carriage was crawling. Outside, cows brushed past, mooing and lowing. Polly pushed down the window and craned her neck. Men and women with pails of water were rushing along the road. "I can see the smoke," she cried.

"Stay calm," said Lady Marchwell.

But Lord Henry flung open the door, pushing against the cattle that were in the way. "Quick, Jack, quick, boy," he shouted, grabbing Jack's hand and pulling him out into the melee. Glancing back, Jack saw Polly climbing out too.

"Be careful," cried Tom Drum from the top of the stationary carriage.

Smoke swirled through the autumn air. They could see the house at the end of the road. Smoke was sliding out of the kitchen window and was then swept up in the wind. A brisk wind would fan the flames, thought Jack. Men and women with buckets

182

were dashing in with their full pails and then coming out again, coughing and choking. The pigs had been released and were squealing and screaming as they ran around the square.

"It's got ahold," shouted one man as Jack and Henry ran toward the house.

"Get back!" cried a woman. "There's nothing you can do."

"Come on," cried Henry as they came to the door. Inside, the house was full of smoke, yellow flames licking the wooden frame.

But Jack held back. "You never go into a fire," he shouted.

Lord Henry shook Jack by the arm. "You must go in, to go back," he said urgently. "If the thatch catches, then you will be stuck. You might be stuck forever. You may never go back to your time, where you belong. There is still a way in. You must go."

"But I cannot go in."

"You must."

"You never, ever go back into a fire. That is the rule. You stay away from it. Even if you've left a pet behind."

"You *have* to go back," shouted Lord Henry, pulling him toward the house. "Who knows what may happen if you do not go back?"

"But what about you?"

"I will stay. I belong here. And what will be, will be."

"Try, Jack, you must try," cried Polly.

Grabbing a bucket of water from a man, Lord Henry threw it over Jack and, wrapping his cloak around Jack's shoulders, he pulled him in.

Together they charged through the smoke and up the rickety stairs. Lord Henry kicked open the door into the small bedroom. Jack's eyes were stinging and weeping, and his throat was in pain. The small room had less smoke in it, as the fire was below. Coughing violently, Lord Henry paused and embraced Jack. He struggled with something on his finger and suddenly pressed a ring into Jack's hand.

"I had it from my mother. It is for you now," he told him. "Now quick—go back where you belong." Jack ducked down and found the metal plate that covered the hole through to his bedroom. He pulled it open and saw his room on the other side.

"Good-bye, Jack," called Lord Henry. "Good-bye! Remember me."

The cupboard door closed, as a plume of smoke blossomed into Granny's guest bedroom. Jack lay sprawled on the floor, spewed out of the eighteenth century like a fish upon the shore.

Jack lay there panting, listening to the now-muffled cries coming from the time of the highwaymen. He staggered over to the window and looked out. It was morning. Cars were in the street. The Cap and Stockings was still there, all quiet now, with its neat paintwork and hanging baskets. The fire was out. Or more accurately, he thought, there was no fire in his time.

He went back to the hole in the wall and listened. The cries were still there on the other side; people were calling for more water. Only then he heard a crash. It was followed by a crackle that made his skin prickle with fear. The fire had spread up to the first floor. He felt the iron door. It was hot.

He waited. Was he safe here? He glimpsed himself in the mirror and stared.

His face was black. His eyes were red. His hair was sticking up. His clothes—well, sacking, really—were grimy and wet. He looked as if he had been dragged backward through all the hedges between here and London.

And his room. What a catastrophic mess.

The clock said 8:33. Granny would be up soon.

He listened intently to the wall, imagining the fire on the other side. Slowly he became aware of a silence. He imagined the house burned to the ground. Would the hole into Nanny Manners's house now open into thin air?

It was still early, so he went to the bathroom and ran himself a bath. He scrubbed himself and washed in the warm water and felt refreshed by the luxury of it. On his way out, he came face-to-face with Granny in her robe.

She gave him a strange look.

"Feeling better?" she asked slowly.

"A bit tired," Jack mumbled.

"Speak up!"

"TIRED," he said.

"I should think you are, all that coming and going in the night. Halloween? More like the twelve dancing princesses here! All in army boots! Back to bed. I'm going to bring you breakfast in half an hour."

Jack opened his mouth to object.

"BED!" she boomed.

Jack returned to his room. He looked around. Mud, smoke, soot, candle grease, and pieces of plaster lay everywhere. There were footprints and hand marks all over the wallpaper by the hole in the wall. What could he do? Face the music. It was the only way. He would have to tell Granny. He would start by apologizing. Later, he might be able to show her the way through to the eighteenth century.

Granny came up the stairs and walked into his room. *His* room. There was no need to tell her now. She stopped in the doorway and blinked. Jack waited for the breakfast tray to crash to the floor. Granny seemed frozen. Astonished, amazed, horrified.

But she managed to hold on to the tray. She picked her way over to his bed, avoiding the blankets, pieces of broken chair, and the dirty footprints, and placed the tray of breakfast on Jack's lap.

"Golly," she said finally.

Jack waited for the explosion. But grannies are stalwart and strong. They've seen more of life and its strange twists and ups and downs than children ever give them credit for. She sighed deeply and surprised him.

"What an irresponsible old fool I am," she said, "letting you run about on an adventure. At least you're in one piece. That's the important thing." She shook her head and turned to go.

"Granny." Jack called her back. "I am sorry—and I'll pay for all the damage." His eyes fell on the ring

Lord Henry had given him.

"We'll talk about it later," said Granny briskly. "Now sleep."

Later in the afternoon, as dusk was falling, Jack woke up. He got out of the noisy bed with a loud boinggggg! and, ignoring the ruined room, went straight to the hole in the wall. He felt it.

It was cool. The fire must be out. He peeled back the wallpaper and looked.

The iron door had gone. There was only brick. Solid, immovable brick.

And he realized the eighteenth century had gone too. Suddenly it was as far out of reach as it ever had been. Gone. And with it his friends, and their lives—all on the edge of change. But he wanted to know how they had lived. Did Lord Henry stop robbing and marry Lady Marchwell? Did Polly become a farmer? Did the highwaymen give up robbery?

He felt as if a book had closed and good friends had been lost, and now he must return to his life.

Downstairs, the night was closing in. He went to the kitchen and found Granny there surrounded by donation boxes for the blind. She smiled at him.

"Feel better?" she asked.

"Much better, thanks," Jack replied. He looked out at a group of people standing outside the Cap and Stockings. They were talking animatedly. Granny followed his eyes.

"Something strange has happened at the Cap and Stockings," she said. "Mr. Harrison is very angry. It seems that someone has carved something in the beams, some message or something, and it looks like it is as old as the pub itself yet no one has ever noticed it. It is quite incredible. A superb example of eighteenth-century graffiti. He said it would specially interest us. I said we'd go over later. Jack? Jack!"

Jack had run out of the kitchen. Dodging deftly past the group standing outside, past the man with the camera and the guy with the notebook, he slipped into the pub and looked up at the beams.

First he saw the words "Marchwell" and "Bernard" and then "Henry Vane" and "1753" and then "1770." They were etched into the old oak beams in letters of different sizes—some big, some small. The carvings were dark brown and hardened with time. A woman took him by the arm.

"Come to see the carvings, have you, love? Look,

190

it starts over here." It was the landlady. "We can't think how we've missed it! It's like all this stuff just popped up overnight. The local TV station might be coming later."

Jack read:

To Jack Bolt. No more robbin', no more card games, no more pistols. Henry Vane is my name, being a good husband is my game. Married to Emily Marchwell Nov. 17, 1753. Maid of honor Polly Carter. Celebrated this day in the Cap and Stockings Inn, proprietors Peter Purkins, Bernard Belch, Dick Willowherb.

On another beam was written:

We miss you, Jack Bolt. And we think of you oftentimes. Wondering what happened to you. Polly Swann, 17 heifers, 14 acres, 3 babies. 1770.

Jack read the carvings three times. Now he knew. Lives summed up in a few sentences. The door into Nanny Manners's house had never opened again. Not in their lifetimes. They were long gone now. They were long dead and buried.

Yet only yesterday . . .

He left the pub as more people were coming in. But instead of going home he went over to the churchyard. He could picture the highwaymen still, standing idly over the gravestones. The graveyard was changed, he thought. There was an old headstone that tilted beside the path. He could have sworn it wasn't there the day before when they had all been eating breakfast here. Yet there it was, now covered with moss and lichen. He bent down to read the inscription:

Here Lies
Lord Henry Vane
Magistrate
1729 – 1789
&
Lady Emily Vane
1732 – 1793
United in peace.